CW00469591

TRACK DOWN AFRICA

A Brad Jacobs Thriller

<u>Book 1</u>

SCOTT CONRAD

Scott Conrad's "A Brad Jacobs Thriller" Series takes retired Force Recon Marine Brad Jacobs and his fellow veterans on dangerous and thrilling international search, rescue and hostage retrieval expeditions. Their missions are to "Track Down" and retrieve innocent victims by facing off against fierce, powerful enemies and extremely challenging conditions.

Enjoy the non-stop action, adventure and mystery with the entire team as they always manage to keep their sense of humor even during the riskiest of operations. Each book is a complete story on its own.

A Brad Jacobs Thriller Series by Scott Conrad:

TRACK DOWN AFRICA – BOOK 1

TRACK DOWN ALASKA – BOOK 2

TRACK DOWN AMAZON – BOOK 3

TRACK DOWN IRAQ – BOOK 4

TRACK DOWN BORNEO – BOOK 5

TRACK DOWN EL SALVADOR – BOOK 6

TRACK DOWN WYOMING – BOOK 7

TRACK DOWN THAILAND – BOOK 8

Visit the author at: ScottConradBooks.com

"A Marine is a Marine. I set that policy two weeks ago - there's no such thing as a former Marine. You're a Marine, just in a different uniform and you're in a different phase of your life. But you'll always be a Marine because you went to Parris Island, San Diego or the hills of Quantico. There's no such thing as a former Marine."

General James F. Amos, 35th Commandant of the Marine Corps

Table of Contents

PROLOGUE

The Central African Republic rests uneasily in the center of a lousy neighborhood. The country occupies 240,000 square miles. It is bordered by Chad and Sudan to the north, the Democratic Republic of the Congo and the Congo to the south, a long and war-torn border with southern Sudan to the east, and Cameroon to the west. More than 4.5 million souls live in this landlocked country. Despite its substantial mineral deposits, uranium reserves, gold, diamonds, lumber, oil, hydroelectric power, and large quantities of rich farmland, it's one of the world's ten most destitute countries.

The period between 1960, when the CAR gained its independence from France, and 2003, when its first democratically elected president, Ange-Félix Patassé, was ousted by General François Bozizé, had been scarred by civil unrest under a series of autocratic rulers.

A year after Bozizé seized power, the Central African Republic Bush War started, pitting the government, the Christian majority, and the fifteen percent of the population that is Muslim (the Séléka) against each other. Despite peace treaties in 2007 and 2011, fighting again broke out between the warring factions in 2012. The result has been massive population dislocation due to religious and ethnic cleansing. A Christian majority has banded together with ex-soldiers, Christians and animists (people who believe, among other things, that magic will protect them from bullets) to form militias known as anti-balaka, which in the local Sango language means "anti-machete".

The political situation in the CAR remains both perilous and tenuous and can be described at best as very fluid. Conflicting reports come from the area daily, hinting at the possibility of an imminent solution to the troubles afflicting the beleaguered people of the CAR. Experts remain skeptical.

MISSING – Day One

It was 2240 hours when Brad Jacobs stepped off the aircraft at Dallas/Fort Worth International Airport, passed through the jetway and then checked his voicemail. The retired Marine drew admiring glances from several female passersby.

At thirty-seven, Jacobs was six feet two, with a muscular build and a blond buzz cut. He had a lantern jaw and a look of self-confidence in his green eyes. His unconscious military bearing showed a core of inner strength in the man, a core built from courage, from facing the toughest obstacles life could put in his way.

He had just returned from Las Vegas where he had tracked down and retrieved a bail jumper. There was only one message in his voicemail, an urgent one from Jack Paul, his uncle. The man sounded frantic, mumbling something nearly unintelligible about trouble with his daughter Jessica.

His brow wrinkled with concern. He and Jessica had grown up together, and she was more like a little sister than a cousin. She was the only family member who had stayed in close contact with him during his fifteen years in the military, sending him cards on his birthdays and letters liberally doused in outrageous perfumes with bright red lipstick kisses on the envelopes. She'd overheard him teasing a buddy once, about getting letters like that at mail call. She found it hilarious to imagine Brad's embarrassment when he received one of his own. He had taken a great deal of ribbing from his buddies over the years. Jessica also sent him care packages with cookies and cakes to share with his friends when he had been deployed overseas. They were poignant reminders of home and normality, and they helped Brad and his buddies through the hard and lonely times. They had grown even closer during the four years since his discharge with frequent visits to each other's houses. If she were really in some sort of trouble there was no question that he would drop everything to help her.

Brad Jacobs had grown up as a loner, an only child. It seemed as if his father was continually being transferred to different bases. There was never enough time to build many long-term friendships. After attending his fourth school in five years, he gave up trying to make friends. When his dad had been posted to what was to be his final deployment in Iraq, Brad and his mom went to live with wealthy Uncle Jack, his mom's brother.

After his father died, they continued living with Jack Paul until Brad enlisted in the Marine Corps. It was during the four years of living with his uncle that Brad had grown to love Jessica as if she were his sister. Nothing was more important to him than protecting her. Now, all he could think about was getting his belongings and getting to a quiet place where he could call Jack and find out what was going on.

Brad enlisted in the Corps immediately after graduating high school. The career choice seemed to be a natural fit for the young man. His father, Lou Jacobs, had been a career Marine who'd died at the end of the First Gulf War during Operation Desert Storm while serving under Lt. General Walter E. Boomer, the Marine Force Commander for General Norman Schwarzkopf. Brad was proud of his dad, and a proud, firm believer in what the Marines stood for. It was his pride, integrity, and desire to excel that led him to volunteer for Force Recon, the elite among the already elite Marine Corps. He'd spent the last ten years of his career as one of the best of the best. Three times he'd deployed to Iraq, fighting in the Second Battle of Fallujah and actively taking part in the search for Saddam Hussein.

Since his separation from the Corps, he'd worked as a private military contractor, which he'd hated, and then he'd changed his focus. He'd become a specialist in tracking down and locating missing persons who disappeared while in dangerous countries that traditional law enforcement tended to avoid. He always enlisted help on these missions from a select pool of men he trusted and had previously served with. His reputation had grown over time. He'd eventually started working as a hostage retrieval expert for international corporations to retrieve high-level executives who had been abducted in foreign countries. In between jobs, he used his skills as a bounty hunter to keep busy. He didn't love the bounty hunter work, but it kept his skills honed and sharp for when he really needed them to find missing persons.

* * *

He called his uncle immediately as he exited the airport. Jack picked up on the first ring.

"What's going on with Jessica?" Brad asked.

"She's three days late checking in with me."

Jessica was a treasure hunter, always looking to find a fortune. At twenty-six she didn't really need the money, but she enjoyed the chase and the adventures. Her father had long before established a trust fund that left her quite comfortable after she came of age, though the fund had restrictions and conditions that limited how she could spend it. Jack was a devious man, a control freak who couldn't bear the idea of Jessica's independent nature. Although desperate to make her own fortune, she wasn't yet willing to relinquish the semi-lavish lifestyle Jack and his trust fund provided. There was one rule she never broke because compliance assured her father's continued support in her efforts to make her own way—the weekly check-in call. Brad knew immediately that his cousin was in trouble. Over the years, he and Jessica had learned how to keep the peace with Jack. And abiding by his wishes, no matter how self-indulgent, was an important aspect.

"Where is she this time?" Brad asked.

"The Central African Republic."

"Jesus, what the hell is she doing in the CAR?" Brad paused at the curb as he looked for a taxi in the freezing rain. Usually there was a line of the damned things waiting for recent arrivals, but the weather seemed to have generated a greater demand for them on this wintry night.

"Looking for a lost diamond mine," Jack continued.

"You've gotta be kidding me, doesn't she know that the Séléka Rebels control most of that country?"

"You know Jessica, not afraid of a damned thing."

More like crazy, Brad thought. *You do everything you can to run her life, Uncle Jack, why in the hell did you let her go to the CAR of all places?* He knew there was no time for recriminations, so he cleared his mind and concentrated on what it would take to bring Jessica back.

Brad's fifteen years as a Force Recon Marine and his vocation over the following four years had given him the skills needed to find people and to deal with trouble. He'd need all those skills to find Jessica. He also knew from personal experience that the CAR was one of the most dangerous places on the planet, and operations there were a logistical nightmare. Getting himself into the country was going to be a serious challenge, never mind finding Jessica and getting her out.

"So," Brad asked, "where exactly was she in the CAR the last time you spoke with her?"

"When she checked in last week," Jack replied, "she was somewhere east of Bangui, in the southern prefecture of Kemo, following research on Henry Morton Stanley and his last African expedition in 1887. Somewhere she read a legend of Stanley's party stumbling onto an immense diamond mine hidden in the jungle near the Ubangi River. She was trying to follow a map she discovered concealed in the binding of one of Stanley's old diaries. She told me that the diary appeared to be in his handwriting. I asked if she'd had it authenticated, but she wouldn't discuss it with me."

Jack's voice sounded strained as he continued. "She sensed they were getting close to the location indicated on the map, but she felt like someone was tracking them."

"Them?" Jack asked. "Who was with her?"

"All she told me was two research assistants she'd worked with before, and a couple of local guides. She never told me their names, so I have no way of tracking them. She went on to say that small rebel patrols harassed them a couple times, but she wasn't convinced they were the ones tracking her party. She said they traveled so deeply into the jungle she thought they probably lost whoever was behind them."

Shit! That frigging jungle is as bad as the Congo. I've known experienced trackers to get hopelessly lost in that hellhole! "Okay, I'll take care of it," Brad replied. "Let me know if you come up with any more information, Uncle Jack. It's gonna be a long night."

Brad disconnected the call as he finally flagged down a taxi. He'd been exhausted when he'd landed at the airport, and waiting around for an hour for the cab had made it worse, but he knew there'd be no rest for him this night. The last thing he could afford to think about was sleep.

BAD THOUGHTS, BAD DREAMS

The news about Jessica's disappearance was devastating. Brad realized time would be critical in this situation. Getting to the Central African Republic as quickly as possible was of paramount importance. He knew the CAR far better than he wanted to and knew he could find Jessica. The real

12

question was whether he would be able to find her before that fucking hell on earth killed her.

She could not have found a worse place to get into trouble. There are a million ways to disappear in the middle of Africa, some voluntary, most of a far more sinister nature. There was no way to know if she had been injured, murdered, lost in the jungle, or kidnapped, either for ransom or because some religious fanatic or group didn't like the way she dressed. The rape of a helpless woman was commonplace, and it was not unusual to find the bones of missing people scattered around the jungle floor, bearing the distinct marks of human teeth. Brad thought that being eaten was a thoroughly disgusting way to die and didn't even want to think about that possibility. It was hard to get the mental image of Jessica being chopped up and cooked over an open fire out of his head, no matter how hard he tried. He felt sick to his stomach.

No question he needed backup if he planned on going into the dark heart of Africa. The Séléka was a collection of downright crazy bastards who would be eager to kill him on sight for no reason, and the anti-balaka resented and resisted any outside interference. Brad was a firm believer in peace through superior firepower and he needed a small but decidedly badass team to ensure that both he and Jessica got out of Africa alive.

As he climbed out of the taxi at his apartment near Dallas/Fort Worth International Airport, he pressed the speed dial number on his smartphone to connect him with his closest friend and associate, Mason Ving. Ving was a retired forty-seven-year-old Force Recon gunnery sergeant, a massive man, six feet tall and two hundred and sixty pounds of muscle, tendons, and bones.

Ving had acquired a small beer gut since his retirement from the Corps, but it hadn't slowed him down much. He had skin so black it had blue highlights in the light of day and a bald head that glistened. His smiling brown eyes could turn deadly and reptilian when he got riled, and Brad learned over the years that when Ving's eyes frosted over it was best to be somewhere else.

That's not to say that Ving couldn't be friendly. He had a deep, warm voice that wasn't at all what one would expect to hear coming from the mouth of a Force Recon gunnery sergeant; he sounded like the actor James Earl Jones. When he did get upset, that same voice could sound as if it were issuing from the lungs of Lucifer himself, but that was a rare occurrence. His sheer size and commanding presence were intimidating enough to be more than adequate for most circumstances, even in the most extreme of combat situations.

Brad and Ving served together on many missions including Operation Enduring Freedom in Afghanistan and the Iraq War. They fought together at the Second Battle of Fallujah, known as

Operation Phantom Fury, which was the bloodiest confrontation of the entire Iraq War and the most intense urban warfare involving the Marines since the 1968 Battle of Hue City in Vietnam. Ving had been awarded the Navy Cross for his act of heroism in this battle. Brad had just been happy to come out of it with his ass in one piece.

After retiring from the Corps, the two men became closer than ever. Brad relied on Ving's support on several very heavy assignments in recent years and knew the man would respond to his request in this case. Ving had eaten the lion's share of the cookies and cakes Jessica had sent and he understood the depth of Brad's relationship with his cousin. Brad smiled to himself, remembering Ving's assistance in getting Jessica out of trouble on a couple of her previous escapades.

MOVING FORWARD

Ving barely had a chance to get the phone to his ear before he heard Brad's voice, cold and hard. "Ving, I need your help."

"Dude, it's zero dark thirty and you're callin' askin' for help? What's up, man?"

"It's Jessica, Ving. She's three days late checking in with Uncle Jack."

"I'm guessin', 'cause you ain't laughin' that she ain't laid up on some beach in the Caribbean with some male model," Ving grumbled. He knew Jessica was a little prone to getting into a jam now and then, but it was easy to forgive her because she was pretty and she made some damned fine chocolate chip cookies . . . his favorite kind. Ving sat upright in his bed, fully awake and alert but speaking quietly so as not to disturb his wife. "Where was she when she last made contact, Brad?"

"The CAR," Brad replied.

"Oh shit! Couldn't she find a more dangerous place to play?" Ving grunted. "What's the plan?"

"That's why I'm calling, Ving. I need you to put together a search plan, work out logistics, and get us and a small team on the ground in Bangui by tomorrow night."

"No fuckin' way, Brad," Ving barked. "You know that the CAR is one of the most difficult places in the entire damn world to get into. Even with our contacts it could take at least three or four days just to get the visas. And you can forget about trying to get permits to bring in weapons. There ain't no way. And you'd have to be fuckin' nuts to go into that country without weapons. Come to think of it, I must be crazy too, for even seriously considerin' goin' with you! Listen, why don't you start by contacting the local authorities over there and have them search for her? It's seven hours later there; you can probably get someone on the phone right now."

"What authorities?" Brad fumed. "You know as well as I do that the local government there is dysfunctional. Even the American Embassy in Bangui has suspended operations because of the security situation. The Séléka rebels are running roughshod over that country now and the anti-balaka are running around blowing up anything the rebels aren't. The government is bunkered up and praying to last just one more day. I can't contact them; hell, they might even be the ones who have her."

Ving felt the grave concern in Brad's voice deep in the pit of his gut, but he wasn't going to sugarcoat anything for his friend. It wouldn't accomplish a damned thing and Brad would recognize it for the bullshit it was. "Sorry Brad, but hitting the ground tomorrow is not an option. An operation like this takes time to set up. I can get moving on it, and you know I'll give it my best, but I'm gonna need more than just a few hours, brother."

The silence at the other end of the call made Ving hesitate for a moment before dropping the happy bomb on his best buddy. "You know there is one more option, but I'm reluctant to mention it, seein' as how you're always so all-fired insistent on following the rules and such as that. We could go in black. I'm pretty sure I could get us on the ground tomorrow with a shitload of ordnance if you don't mind bendin' a few major international laws and pissin' off everybody from the Congo to the White House.... You do realize how much risk that's gonna add. And it's gonna cost a shit pot full of money."

"Just do it, Mason," Brad said firmly. "I didn't want to make this a clandestine operation, but I have no intention of sitting here with my thumb up my ass when I know Jessica is in deep shit. I have a really bad feeling about this, my brother, and you and I both know that time is critical. I don't give a fuck about the expense; Jack is loaded and I'm good for it even if Jack doesn't pay."

"Yeah, I know man. Look, how many men do you think we're gonna need? You haven't given me much to go on."

"Just four of us," Brad said immediately, "you, me, Pete and Jared."

Pete and Jared were also retired Recon Marines, men who served with Brad and Ving both separately and together. Jared was a highly decorated sniper, probably the most skilled man with a Barrett .50 that Ving had ever seen . . . and he'd seen the best the Corps and the Army had to offer. Pete was a pilot who could fly just about anything, a freak with some C-4 and detonators, as well as a pretty damned good shooter.

Ving had expected Brad would want them along on this mission, but he was a little concerned that his buddy planned to waltz into the hellish nightmare of the CAR with such a small team. It meant that the price of the small arms and explosives just went through the roof. He did recollect however, where he could get his hands on a couple of very expensive prototype M4A1s that had been supplied with heavy bull barrels and suppressors. "Okay brother, I'm on it. I'll get back to you by 0600."

"Roger that," Brad said before he realized that Ving had already hung up. He shivered from the cold as he tucked the cell phone into his coat pocket, and as he bent to lift his duffel bag from the ground where the cab driver had dropped it, he noticed a dark car across the street. What made it so noticeable was a plume of exhaust smoke rising from the tailpipe. There appeared to be someone sitting inside it, but Brad couldn't get a clear look. He turned, lifting the bag, and walked in the front door of his apartment building.

Once inside, he glanced at his wristwatch and noted that it was already 0200 hours. He fumbled in his pocket for the key to his apartment then unlocked door. Tossing the duffel bag to the floor in the kitchen to his left, Brad crossed the living room, picked up a pair of light sensitive Zeiss binoculars and hurried to his window. Parting the drapes, he spotted the dark car, still parked across the street with its motor running.

Brad had no idea who would be watching his apartment building, or why, but it made him uncomfortable as hell. He reached for a pad and pencil and scribbled down the license plate. It was possible that the guy was just some poor dumb private investigator keeping an eye on an errant wife or husband, but it wasn't in Brad's nature to be less than thorough. He tried to get a better look at the car's occupant, but the binoculars were only so good. He couldn't tell who or how many people were inside. He sighed, impatient to get on with his plans. He didn't have time to be fucking around with some unfortunate private dick. He had more important things on his mind.

There was still one more call to make. He desperately needed more information, preferably up to date, on Jessica and what she was doing in deepest, darkest Africa. There was one other person who might have that information, and if he were planning to head into central Africa to find her, Brad was going to have to wake her up despite the miserable hour. If anyone had heard from Jessica it would be Sarah Parks, a diminutive brunette who was Jessica's best friend. They usually spoke daily no matter where the hell Jessica had gone off to, and Jessica kept no secrets from her. Brad's call would more than likely upset her, but it couldn't be helped.

Brad fumbled through his personal contacts list on his cell until he found Sarah's number. The clock on his wall said it was nearly 0230, but he dialed the number anyway. The phone rang five times and went to voicemail. Frustrated, Brad left an urgent message for Sarah to call him regarding Jessica.

He took another look out the window. The drizzling rain had stopped, and the car was gone. His head ached and his eyes were raw and gritty from lack of sleep; he'd been up for more than three days chasing that sorry bastard in Vegas. Brad decided to unpack his duffel bag and start packing for the mission. He sat in his recliner to make a list of things he'd need.

The last time he'd been in central Africa he'd been dropped off in the Democratic Republic of the Congo, where a terrorist group with the unlikely name of "The Lord's Resistance Army", led by a maniac named Joseph Krony, had been joyfully creating havoc, murdering, raping, pillaging, and abducting children. When his commander had briefed Brad's platoon for the "Sting Ray", or direct action, mission, he had warned them that elements of the LRA employed some rather grim methods in their efforts to drive people from their villages. "Don't worry about waxing these geeks if they get in your way. They're not human. They've been known to force the inhabitants of a village to watch them as they make a picnic of one of the smaller children. It takes a special kind of savage to eat a living child in front of its own mother." Their mission had been to recover a codes specialist from the embassy in Kinshasa who had fallen prey to one of the bolder militia groups and been dragged through the jungles to a place near Buta in Orientale Province. Brad thought the lieutenant had been exaggerating. He had not. Of all the horrible sights he had beheld, the actions of the LRA in the heart of the Democratic Republic of the Congo were the things that gave him nightmares. Every species of poisonous reptile, every poisonous insect, every deadly plant, every imaginable disease known to man not only existed in the DRC, it *thrived*. To Brad, if there had ever been a place on Earth that would have profited from being turned into a nuclear wasteland, it was the DRC.

The memories swept through his tired and tortured mind like wildfire, and after a few moments of fighting to clear them, Brad succumbed to his exhaustion. His eyes fluttered and then closed. He slept . . . and he *dreamed*.

THE MISSION – Day Two

Mason Ving sipped from his mug of steaming black coffee and glanced at the clock on his kitchen wall. It was 0500 and he'd been working steadily since Brad called. He was reminded of when he was just a kid and had to get up in the middle of the night to run his newspaper route.

Ving had grown up in a shotgun house in the Central City district of New Orleans, and his mom died when he was barely twelve years old. The oldest of three brothers, he had taken the paper route to help his dad put food on the table. The Marine Corps seemed to be his salvation, so he left home at eighteen to escape the hard life of poverty and to help support his family. Those days were long behind him now. If someone had told him then that someday he might own a home in a nice neighborhood in Fort Worth, Texas, be married to the woman of his dreams, and have two great kids, he would have laughed in their face.

Both Pete Sabrowski and Jared Smoot were on board. The moment Ving told them that Brad's cousin Jessica was in trouble they jumped at the opportunity to help. Even when Ving mentioned that they would be heading for the CAR, neither flinched, although all three of them had been on the "Sting Ray" mission to the DRC with Brad.

Working out the rest of the mission was proving more difficult. He had run into a couple dead ends attempting to secure immediate transportation into the area. At the moment, he was trying to reach Hank Guzman. Hank was an old military intelligence and logistics buddy that Ving had known for over twenty years. He had worked for the CIA and two other government agencies he was not allowed to talk about. Hank kept busy doing freelance work these days but had all the right contacts in all the right places. The man was the best Black Ops specialist Ving had ever known.

Ving was relieved when Hank finally answered the phone. It had been a while since they'd last spoken, and Ving had been hoping against hope that the phone number he had for Hank was still good. After apologizing for waking the man up so early in the morning, Ving explained exactly what they needed including transportation, weapons, and support, and why they needed it.

"I've got some bad news for you, my friend," Hank said. "There is no covert activity or any other activity of any kind in the CAR right now. The place is off-limits. All we have are aerial photographs and satellite feeds to tell us what's happening there. Hell, the CIA has doubled the size of its CAR section, because it got so hot there that they pulled all the spooks out of the country and put them to observing from Langley. It's official—the State Department has certified the entire damned country as a lunatic zone. I hear they're keeping a super close eye on events in Bangui. Hell, the whole world is watching all of Central Africa right now. The instability in the region has a lot of countries very, very nervous."

"The best I can do," he continued, "is get you into the Democratic Republic of Congo. From there you'd be on your own."

"How close to the border and how soon?" Ving asked.

"If you're serious about committing suicide brother, give me fifteen minutes and I'll call you back," Hank replied.

Ving's house was a lot noisier in the early morning than Brad's. His family loved to get up early. It was close to 0600 hours and he knew his boys would be getting up soon. He wanted to get the mission plan set before breakfast. Right on schedule the phone rang.

"Okay," Hank said, "you're good to go. It's going to cost you, though. Make sure to wire the funds to my offshore account before you leave. Just in case."

"Don't worry," Ving responded, "we got you covered. Give me the account and bank routing numbers." Hank read the numbers slowly and clearly.

"You ready to copy?" Hank asked when he was through.

"Roger that."

"I managed to get you a 'space available' hop on a transport, a C-17 out of JRB Naval Air Station Fort Worth Joint Reserve Carswell, departing at 1600 hours today," Hank said. "They are taking supplies to a Navy SEAL unit in Sudan. There are no other scheduled hitchhikers, so you don't need to worry about getting bumped, there's plenty of room. They agreed to make an unscheduled stop en route at a large airstrip in Gemena, DRC. From there you'll need to arrange local transport into the CAR, I don't have any ground resources in Gemena. You are cleared for four men, and I'll have the weapons and other ordnance you requested already loaded on the plane." He stopped as if to take a breath.

"Did you have any trouble getting those prototype M4A1s I asked about?"

"Hell no, but those fuckers are pricey, my friend. He was kinda glad to get rid of them."

"We're gonna be glad to have them."

"I sure hope so, Ving. Say, you guys are taking enough stuff to start a small war. Are you sure this mission is worth the trouble?"

"It is to Brad, and that makes it important to me, Hank."

"Well, good luck to you, and good hunting brother. Stay chilly!"

"Thanks Hank," Ving replied. "I owe you."

"Just send me the money." Hank chuckled.

SARA'S SECRET

At precisely 0600 the phone rang, jolting Brad from a deep sleep.

He shook his head, trying to clear the fog from his brain as he listened to Ving's deep voice telling him that the arrangements had all been made for their departure.

"You sound kind of groggy, buddy," Ving said.

"I am. I was sitting here making a list of what I needed to pack, and I fell asleep."

"From what you said about that Vegas job, I'm thinking you needed the rest, brother."

"Didn't do me much good, Ving. I had nightmares about the last time we were in the DRC."

"That's some bad stuff, brother man. I got over it, but sometimes Willona wakes me up in the night, says I'm yellin' and cryin'. I've never really talked to her about it, but she's a good woman, Brad. She's got my back."

"The best kind," Brad said. Willona was five years Ving's junior, and she had lived in the same neighborhood in Central City that he had grown up in. She was small and pretty but feisty as hell and one-hundred percent loyal to her massive husband and their two boys.

"She's cooking my bacon right now," Ving said. "That woman knows I love me some bacon!"

"Everybody knows you love bacon, Ving!" Brad laughed. Ving's hunger for bacon had been legendary in the Corps. It was a rare mess sergeant who wasn't aware of Master Sergeant Mason Ving's sincere desire to have the cured strips of pork loin for his morning repast and the ways he tended to manifest his extreme displeasure when none was made available to him.

They wasted no more time gabbing, and as soon as Brad hung up the phone, he picked it up again and dialed Jack's number. He really didn't like his Uncle Jack very much, which made him a little ashamed. Jack Paul might well be involved in some slightly shady business dealings, though Brad had never seen any proof, but he had treated Brad and his mother very kindly after Brad's father died in Iraq.

"Are you awake?" he asked.

"I am now." Jack sounded as if Brad had awakened him from a sound sleep, which would have pissed him off if he hadn't fallen asleep himself. It was hard to fault a guy for doing what he himself had done.

"Okay, Uncle Jack," Brad said, "I need a hundred and forty grand wired into my account no later than 1500 today. We'll be wheels up at 1600 hours."

"That much," Jack replied. "That's a lot more than I expected. And that's not much time. My banks aren't even open yet. I may need a couple days to get that much cash together."

Brad was surprised and more than a little angry at Jack's ridiculous response. Jack Paul started out in business with a small salvage yard that he had turned into the largest supplier of used auto parts in the state of Texas. The operation had grown so vast over the years that there were branches from Arizona to Mississippi, and around the world, and they all did a huge cash business. Brad worked in one of the larger yards outside Fort Worth to make spending money as a kid, and he had never known that one yard to have less than a hundred thousand dollars in cash in the safe on premises. Jack even lectured him about it when he'd seen the open door of the big double door safe with the words "Trumbull Safe & Vault Co., Chicago U.S." printed on the front in faded gold leaf. Jack also kept large accounts at various banks all over the world, particularly ones that weren't subject to U.S. banking laws. He used them to handle his international business transactions, and, Brad strongly suspected, as a place to hide unrecorded cash from the IRS. A guy like Jack could access a hundred and forty thousand dollars in a matter of minutes.

Brad raised his voice only slightly, the anger bleeding through his tone despite his determination to keep his temper in check for Jessica's sake. "Just get it to me as soon as you can, Jack." Brad hung up without saying goodbye, thankful that he hadn't lost his temper. There was no way he was going to let anyone or anything derail this mission. Not with Jessica's safety and possibly her life dependent on him.

Brad forced himself to take several deep breaths and calm down. He needed to stop being melodramatic and assuming the worst. There was no proof that anything terrible had happened to Jessica. *There's no proof that she hasn't been eaten alive by the LRA either,* a vicious voice inside his head argued.

Brad knew the CAR from first-hand experience, and he knew it well. His last four years as a hostage retrieval specialist had been rewarding beyond his wildest dreams, and he had enough money put away to cover the hundred and forty thousand himself, if he accessed his line-of-credit account. He didn't hesitate for even a second. He called Ving back and arranged for the funds transfer from his own account. There would be time to settle up with Jack Paul when Jessica was safe.

The phone rang just as he was breaking the connection with Ving.

It was Sarah Parks. "I got your message, Brad."

"Sarah, God, I'm so glad you called! Listen, when was the last time you spoke to Jessica?"

"About six days ago, why?"

"I'll explain in a minute. Now what exactly did she tell you?"

"Just that she was trying to find a lost cave that contained a legendary diamond mine," Sarah said. "She acquired some kind of map—she found it in a musty old diary that had been passed down to one of Henry Morton Stanley's descendants. She told me she'd had the writing on the map authenticated by an expert over at SMU. It was Stanley's writing…. Brad, what's this all about? You're scaring me!"

"Be patient with me, Sarah. What else did she say?"

"She said she'd experienced minor trouble with the local rebels but not to worry because she could handle it."

Brad sensed that Sarah was holding something back. The seconds were ticking away and he had to get all the information he could before he got on that C-17.

"Sarah, I don't have time for secrets. Jessica missed her weekly check-in call to Jack and you're apparently the last one here to speak with her. No one seems to be able to reach her. She's been off the grid for at least six days and I'm not sure why. She could be lost or hurt, she may have been kidnapped for ransom or someone may be holding her because they think she actually discovered the location of this cockamamie diamond mine, and they want to know what she knows. I'm going after her and if you know something you're not telling me, I need you to spill it right now!"

"Oh my God!" Sarah gasped. "She had another reason for being there, one she didn't want me to tell anyone about, especially you."

"That's too bad, Sarah. You have to tell me."

"Okay . . . she believes her father may have direct ties to the blood diamond trade in Africa."

"What the hell are you talking about, Sarah? She thinks Jack is in business with the Séléka rebels?" Brad felt a leaden ball growing in the pit of his stomach. He was well aware of Jack Paul's expanding international business dealings over the past few years, and he knew from experience that the man was capable of less than ethical business practices . . . but blood diamonds? It was a despicable trade, plied by evil men even more ruthless than the drug barons of Central and South America. The blood diamond traders marched hand in hand with human traffickers and drug lords. He didn't want to believe his uncle Jack could be involved in something like that.

Sarah's voice quivered as she continued. "When Jess was doing her research on this project, she was poking around in her dad's study and found correspondence from an address in the CAR. It wasn't too specific, and most of the information was numbers, but she did see several letters from a man named Ostrigamo. She recognized his name from her earlier research on the CAR as one of the leaders of the Séléka alliance. She had proof that there were definitely some financial transactions between Ostrigamo and her father, but she couldn't or wouldn't tell me the nature of them.... Brad, what are you going to do? Now I'm really worried about her!"

"Sarah, this changes everything. If what you're telling me is the truth, there's more to Jessica's disappearance than I can understand right now. Hell, Ostrigamo may be using her as leverage over Uncle Jack."

"Yeah, that thought crossed my mind, but I didn't want to believe it. But I'm thinking that maybe she found the diamond mine, Brad, and if she did, Ostrigamo knows she found it. There could be more diamonds in that mine than they've been able to pull out of the local rivers in the last ten years. She wouldn't tell me everything, but I could tell from the excitement in her voice that she thought she had uncovered something—something really big."

Really big to Jessica must have been diamonds. When she went on these treasure hunts, the only thing she cared about was finding what she hunted for. Brad scribbled *Ostrigamo* on a notepad, thanked Sarah for her time and hung up. He'd have plenty of time to research the rebel leader on the flight to Africa.

WHEELS UP

It was 1300 hours by Brad's wrist chronometer by the time he left for the air station, and he was still processing what Sarah had told him. His first thought had been that he should delay the mission so he could get a better picture of what was going on. If Sarah had the right of it, Jack's procrastinating about financing the mission made a little more sense, but it put the man in a really bad light. *What the hell was Jessica up to over there? Was she looking for treasure or trying to find out if her father was tied up in some international criminal activity with the Séléka rebels?*

His combat instincts, honed over a lifetime, automatically assumed control of his brain. Things became clearer, his mind became more focused. He was in battle mode.

It didn't matter what the reasons were. Jessica was in over her head, and there was a ninety percent chance she was in mortal danger . . . and those weren't odds Brad was comfortable with. After thinking it over he felt glad he had decided early on to follow his instincts and push this search and rescue mission forward as quickly as possible. It was simply sound tactical decision making at work.

What he needed most was information, and for that he would need boots on the ground in the CAR. The only way to get and verify practical intelligence was to go get it himself. The mission was a go.

* * *

The massive Boeing C-17 Globemaster III aircraft was sitting on the runway like some rough beast when Brad arrived at the Carswell naval air station. Ving, Jared, and Pete were already aboard by the time the base operations guy led Brad onto the tarmac. The freezing rain had stopped, but a cold wind swept across the runway, and the hot jet blast was a welcome relief when Brad got close enough to feel it. The familiar smell of JP-4 hit his nostrils and he felt energized. Despite his hatred of the DRC and the jeopardy his cousin was in, the promise of imminent combat made his blood sing. For a true warrior, it was a feeling akin to sex.

Ving had prepared an operations order, and he was eager to start the briefing. Only the inboard and outboard troop seats were installed. Brad had to walk around the pallets strapped to the deck of the huge aircraft as well as a couple of Humvees.

The crew chief, chattering into his headset, closed the personnel door and the noise from the four F117 Pratt & Whitney jet engines diminished slightly. Brad settled into the seat next to Ving, and Pete and Jared leaned forward in their own seats to maintain eye contact. Ving handed Brad a headset like the ones he and the other two were already wearing, and when he put it on, the engine noises muted to a dull whisper. Ving's voice, however, was clear and deep.

"Okay guys, our objective is obvious. We're here to locate and recover Jessica Paul as safely and with as little fuss as possible while engaging hostiles the least we can manage.

"Our first big challenge will likely be at the airport. The DRC is basically a war zone…. The Tutsi and the Hutu have been fighting each other for decades, and they're the two biggest ethnic factions in this part of Africa.

"The best intel available is that one of the CAR government's top army colonels, a guy named Leupold Gicanda, has recently deserted with several hundred of his troops and joined the ranks of the M23 rebel group. M23 is Tutsi, and they now control the airport at Gemena. Unconfirmed reports from civilian informants indicate that Gicanda has left only a skeleton force at Gemena and deployed to the town of Bumba, some eight hundred miles to the north. We still need to hit the ground at Gemena Airport locked and loaded and ready for a battle because we have no firm idea of their strength or their will to fight. The C-17 won't even come to a full halt; they're going to land with the tailgate down. It's up to us to unass the aircraft before the crew chief tells the pilots to throttle up and take off, which will be one second after our boots hit that tarmac.

"Gemena has a decent sized airport, and according to my sources there should be several helicopters on site. The only satellite photos I could obtain showed a half dozen Vietnam Era Hueys tied down outside the main hangar and a Bell Jet Ranger, so we should be able to get hold of one of them if we don't see any other options. We're either going to co-opt a friendly chopper pilot or Pete here is going to hijack us the best of the birds he can hotwire.

"We will fly to Bangui, nap-of-the-earth the last twenty miles or so. We'll land at an LZ (landing zone) I've selected on the outskirts of Bangui about a half a mile from Bangui M'Poko International Airport, near, oddly enough, one of Jack Paul's salvage yards. Satellite reconnaissance shows an abundance of vehicles at the yard, but the truth is we have no idea how many of them are operable. Sorry I couldn't do any better, but this was done on the fly and I gave it my best shot. We should be able to secure ground transport there, but we'll need a bit of luck to pull this off.

"Once we reach the staging area, we will use ground transport to enter Bangui, get additional intel and an update on what we already know.

"The information I received from my source is that we need to meet up with another confidential informant in Bangui. The Defense Department currently uses this guy for reliable updates on the status of the local political situation. His name is

Carson and he can usually be found at a well-known bar called Madame Maboki's. He's an information broker, collects information and sells to all sides. If anyone knows anything regarding Jessica's whereabouts, Carson would have heard about it."

"Jesus Ving, that sounds pretty thin," Jared remarked. "Why the hell would anybody spread gossip concerning a lone woman?"

"A lone *white* woman, Jared, will be a hot conversation topic anywhere in central Africa. There's no doubt in my mind that many people in Bangui have heard about her, maybe they've even heard where she's at. Our problem is they're not going to talk to us. The only thing these people hate more than they hate each other is the white man."

"Surely they'd talk to you...." Pete said.

"Because I'm black? Dude listen to yourself. I don't speak a word of *Sango* or *Kinyarwanda.* In their book, I'm as white as *you* are."

Brad was laughing. He'd been listening, and he could have explained it to Pete, but it was funny to watch Pete's face as Ving set him straight. The Tutsi and the Hutu possessed a virulent hatred of each other, a hatred that had led to genocidal attacks on both sides . . . all because the Tutsi raised cattle for a living and the Hutu raised crops. It was a class war, pure and simple, but it was ferocious. And Ving was right; the only thing that incensed the Tutsi and the Hutu more than the sight of each other was the sight of a white man.

Ving finished the operations order, just as he would have on a true military operation. There followed a question and answer period that continued until Ving was satisfied that each man knew where he was supposed to be at all times, what his responsibilities were, what weapons and ordnance he was to have in his possession, and how they planned to exfiltrate the CAR once Jessica had been recovered. An operations order was designed to cover every detail of an operation from start to finish and every imaginable contingency. Ving wrote a better op order than most.

As the briefing ended, the C-17 began to taxi toward the runway for takeoff, right on schedule at 1600 hours. After they had broken down the weapons and other ordnance and stowed them on and in their gear, Brad motioned for Ving to remove his headset and walk with him to the back of the cargo area.

Ving followed him, walking alongside the Humvees and the cargo pallets until they were standing between the last pallet and the broad, flat cargo door.

"Do we have clearance to use the communication system on this aircraft?"

"Think I can make that happen," Ving replied with a smile.

"Good," said Brad. "I want you to check for any ties between Uncle Jack and the Séléka rebels' blood diamond trade. Specifically red flag the name Ostrigamo."

"Are you serious?" Ving was shocked.

"Dead serious."

"Oh hell!" Ving muttered, clapping a broad, dark hand to his forehead. "Why do I feel this mission just went to shit?"

GEMENA – Day Three

Ving confirmed a connection between Jack Paul and Ostrigamo just as they were approaching Gemena Airport. It was day three and nearly 1300 hours local time as they circled the runway. His research had shown that Jack made cash withdrawals the same days Ostrigamo had made deposits for the same amounts. He didn't know what the money was for, but he was certain it had something to do with payment for blood diamonds.

"Weapons check," Brad said over the intercom as the massive aircraft banked to the left for the final descent. He knew that the DRC was just as dangerous and unstable as the CAR and he had no idea how many men of M23 would be on the ground waiting for them. However many there might be, they would have been warned of the approach of the military cargo plane by the tower personnel at the airport . . . provided there was anyone manning the tower. This was, after all, Africa. "Our plan is to get in and out of Gemena as quickly as possible," Brad continued. "Check out the choppers as we approach. These guys aren't going to leave this bird on the ground one second longer than they have to." They heard the whine of the cargo door being lowered and felt the inrush of fresh air.

"As soon as it slows down enough to get off, do it. No time for the safety rules, guys, lock and load!" As soon as the giant craft touched down and the thrusters were reversed, the team moved toward the cargo door.

Brad and Ving had developed an unusual relationship over the years. Throughout their time together on active duty, Ving was always the one in charge, the one issuing orders. Since their retirement, however, on all the bounty hunting jobs and other assorted private missions, Brad had been in charge. Their mutual respect made the transition easy. Ving enjoyed helping Brad when he needed it. He liked the excitement of having a job to do and getting it done, and the work made it easier to deal with his boring retirement.

It was a smooth touchdown. The runway at Gemena was 6,549 feet long, and the big C-17 could land in as little as 3,500 feet. The pilots executed a combat landing, braking hard and running the thrust-reversed engines at maximum military power to slow the aircraft to a crawl as quickly as possible. Once Brad and his team stepped off the cargo ramp, the crew chief yelled for the pilots to take off and the door mechanism began to whine as the engines switched back to their normal configuration. Brad looked over his shoulder as the bird took off again, still at maximum military power. He always found it amazing that such a huge aircraft could take off in as little as 600 feet and then climb at such an incredibly steep angle.

Brad spotted four Hueys parked a few hundred yards to the east of the main runway. He ordered Jared to stay with the gear and led Ving and Pete toward the choppers.

"Two armed guards at the chopper line," Pete barked as he scanned the field with his binoculars.

"Are they airport security or Tutsi?" Brad asked as they closed in.

"M23," Pete responded.

At just that moment the soldiers opened fire on them. By the time the three of them had hit the ground, Jared had already picked off the Tutsi with a single head shot each. He had been monitoring the situation through the sniper scope on his personal M40A5. He purchased the weapon after his separation from the Corps and he never went on one of Brad's jobs without it. The kill shots had been made at a dead run, and there had been no hesitation.

Brad knew that the sound of gunfire would have alerted any other Tutsi at the airport, and they had only moments to clear the area before they would risk a confrontation with the remaining Tutsi of M23. The three of them sprinted toward the chopper line with Brad leading the way.

One chopper caught Pete's eye. It was an old Vietnam era UH-1F that had been remanufactured and labeled Huey II, parked at the end of the row. The Huey was one of the most readily recognizable helicopters in the world. After the UH-60 Black Hawk had been adopted by the U.S. military, the UH-1 fleet had been sold or given away to every country in the known world. Thousands of them were produced for the Vietnam War, and the things were so incredibly durable that many were pressed into service without the benefit of refurbishment. There were even companies in the U.S. that specialized in airframe up restorations of the venerable craft. The Huey II was comparably inexpensive, totally reliable, and there was a massive inventory of spare parts. It became the "poor man's" chopper and they were sold everywhere. The Huey became the helicopter equivalent of the Volkswagen Beetle. The one on the flight line had been dressed up and the seats covered with new vinyl; it was obviously the local commander's bird. Pete went toward it at a dead run. He had learned to fly one of these even before he'd gone into the Corps.

There was no time to find a local pilot, and there was no need to. Pete slipped the catch on the right side door and was inside in the seat flipping switches and checking dials. "She's been topped off," he yelled, raising his right hand with his thumb extended upwards, "she's ready to go!" Ving and Brad slid the passenger compartment door back until it locked open and crawled in on the deck. Brad lay on the aluminum deck and took up a firing position while Ving crawled over him to open the opposite door and take up a firing position of his own. Both men watched anxiously for more Tutsi to appear while Pete fired up the engines and the big rotors began to spin. It seemed to take forever before Brad felt the chopper go light on the skids, and then Pete worked the pitch and collective levers as he throttled up. The Huey's ass end picked up first, and then the nose went down as Pete spun the chopper and began a short, low level run toward Jared and the team's pile of gear.

BANGUI – 1800 Hours

Bangui was hot, dirty, and, despite being the capital of the CAR, smelled like a third-world sewer. Brad knew the smell all too well. He had been in at least a dozen cities just like Bangui—dangerous and barbaric, but also full of intrigue, and for the unwary or the unschooled, death. There was a permanent haze in the air.

Most of the buildings and houses were white with corrugated sheet metal roofs. The only real color was in the women's clothes—bright, cheery fabric colors lit up an otherwise dreary landscape. They were here to get information and then get out as quickly as possible. Bangui was situated on the northern banks of the Ubangi River and was known as one of the most dangerous cities in the world. The Muslim Séléka and the nominally Christian Anti-Balaka had battered the inhabitants mercilessly over the past few years, and that was on top of the genocidal depredations of the Tutsi and the Hutu. Large portions of the capital city were in ruins.

As they entered the city Brad felt the old truck sputter and almost die. It was a real heap that Jared had procured from Jack Paul's salvage yard on the outskirts of town—but it had been the best of the ones they had managed to locate. From the information Ving's research had turned up, they knew they were heading for a popular bar known as Madame Maboki's. Looking at the destruction in the streets, Brad wondered if the Muslim Séléka might have demolished the place in their religious fervor. If it were still standing, it would be here they would likely find Carson, the CIA confidential informant who could give them the much needed intel on the possible whereabouts of Jessica.

Fortunately, finding the bar was easy. It was one of the few places on the street that was untouched, speaking much for the influence of the owner and/or Carson. All they had to do now was locate

Carson. The bar was a decidedly unsavory establishment. As they walked through the door the patrons looked up from their drinks through the smoky air with hatred in their eyes, though the bleary eyes were quickly hooded as soon as they noticed the two M4A1s and Jared's sniper rifle. Brad's CAR-4 was too unspectacular to draw as much attention as the other weapons. Ving had gotten an excellent description of Carson, but it turned out to be unnecessary. The black eye patch and the brilliant white shirt and trousers were a dead giveaway. Ving spotted him as they cleared the doorway.

Carson was seated at a relatively clean table, surrounded by large, dark men who greatly resembled Ving. *Tutsi*, Brad thought, *they tend to be on the tall side, considerably taller than the Hutu*.

Ving approached Carson and quietly spoke the code-phrase he had been given. Carson nodded and waved his left hand expansively, indicating that Ving should sit at the table across from him. He waved at the bartender and held up a single finger. The bartender, a short man in a dirty white shirt and pants, shuffled toward the table carrying two green glass bottles of Mocaf beer. Carson didn't even acknowledge Brad or the other two men.

After exchanging a few pleasantries and accepting a stack of crisp, new hundred-dollar bills with the bank bands still wrapped tightly around them, Carson got right to business. He told Ving that Jessica's party had last been seen about two hundred miles east of Bangui. They were reportedly in the jungle near Mobaye, searching for a legendary lost diamond mine. Carson seemed to be amused, shaking his head at what he deemed to be Jessica's folly. "This area happens to be deep in Séléka rebel territory," he said. "Pity no one warned her about the dangers of a woman alone in the middle of the Dark Continent. Surely her father warned her."

Ving gave the man a hard look.

"Oh yes," Carson said with a broad, white smile. "I know her father. He's the only reason you and your friends are still alive and the only reason the fair Jessica wasn't taken as a companion for some of our more prominent citizens."

Ving bit his lip to keep from snarling at the snide son of a bitch, and he prayed Brad didn't lose it either. Ving waited for Carson to continue.

"Anyone searching for diamonds goes through Mobaye," Carson said. "All the diamonds from the CAR come out through Mobaye. I recommend you start there and see a man named Nuru. Nuru is a black marketeer and information broker who knows just about everything that goes on in his small part of the world." His eyes scanned the room before he continued in a lower voice.

"You might also want to talk to a man called Ostrigamo, if you can find him. He is the top rebel leader in this part of the country and most likely the one responsible for the woman's disappearance. If not, he at least knows where she is. I have no idea if Mr. Paul's influence extends that far."

Ving could tell from the man's expression that he damn well knew the connection between Jack Paul and Ostrigamo. "What's the best way to get to Mobaye?"

Carson raised his one good eye to the slowly spinning fan suspended from the ceiling. "There are no commercial flights over this region. Somehow the Séléka managed to acquire a shipment of old Russian SA-7 missiles, and since they figured out how to use them, they've had considerable success in taking out aircraft. They have proven extremely effective against most flights heading into Mobaye.

"That leaves you two ways to get there. Road or river. There's only one road and it has so many

Séléka checkpoints that it's really not an option. That leaves the Ubangi River.

"The river has daytime patrols, so traveling on it at night is your best choice. You are going upriver, so you will need a boat with an engine and a captain who knows the river; both are hard to find but absolutely necessary. Navigation in the dark is challenging on this river because there are several sets of rapids upriver from here. And do remember it's a hundred and fifty nautical miles. That's at least a ten-hour trip at night by boat. Provided you have the right kind of boat."

Carson looked immensely pleased with himself as he lifted his beer bottle toward Ving in a mocking gesture. "I believe our business is concluded."

"I don't think so," Ving growled, leaving his own beer untouched. "How the hell am I going to find a boat to go upriver this time of the evening?"

Carson's smile grew even broader. "That is not my problem, American; boats were not included in our deal."

"My question stands, Carson. Where the hell am I going to find a boat and a captain?" Ving looked as menacing as Brad had ever seen him, but Carson seemed unflappable.

"I suppose, if you could find another stack or two of those hundred-dollar bills, I might be able to secure the necessary items for you." When Carson saw the anger flash across Ving's dark face he shrugged and raised his hands. "A man has to make a living."

Brad stepped forward, lifting a single stack of new hundreds out of his pocket and tossing it on the table. "That's ten grand. That's enough to buy a fleet of boats and captains to drive them in this part of the world."

Carson stared interestedly at the well-stuffed cargo pocket Brad had pulled the stack from. His eyes narrowed. "You are either bold or foolish, white man, to come into my place of business with so much cash and treat me so rudely. I might take offense and relieve you of your burden."

"And I might blow you all to hell if you tried it," Brad replied calmly, casually pulling out a small diameter green metal ball with the letters 'U.S.' stenciled on its smooth round sides. Ving picked up the hand grenade and quickly removed the ring with the pin through it, holding the firing lever tightly against the palm of his hand.

Carson checked Brad's eyes for any sign of a bluff, but all he saw in those hard green eyes was death. His own eyes went to the tiny tattoo on Brad's forearm where it peeked out from beneath his sleeve. It was the Marine Corps globe and fouled anchor emblem with the words "Force Recon" on a banner beneath it. He raised his eyes back to Brad's. "I have seen your kind here before, soldier."

"Not soldier, Carson," Ving said. "Marine."

Carson reached out, carefully avoiding Ving's hand and the grenade in it. "I think I can accommodate you, gentlemen, but it will take me an hour or so."

BOAT LAUNCH

When the small group reached the small river town of Badokwa, it was nearly 2100 hours. Carson, who had led the way in a battered old Volkswagen Thing, explained he had done the best that he could for them. Then he produced a hand-drawn map of the Ubangi, showing the approximate locations of navigation hazards.

Brad was pissed, but he was in a rush to get on the river so they could complete their journey under the cover of night. He followed Carson down to the side of the river and stared in astonishment.

"You've gotta be kidding me. Those look like freaking canoes."

"They're called pirogues," said Carson. "You've got two of them. Each one has a small outboard on the back and a captain, a local guide. Unfortunately, all the larger boats you see in this area are only good for heading downstream in the deeper water. These pirogues are the only boats that can make it through the shallow rapids upstream from here."

"Shit!" Brad cursed. "Ving and I can take the bigger one. Let's get the gear loaded."

"Okay, let's go," Ving barked.

Ving glared dubiously at the small, narrow boats. He wasn't certain he could force his large frame into one. Then he hesitated as he stepped into the larger one. "What swims in this river?" he asked.

"Just crocodiles, Ving," Jared said, laughing.

"Not funny." Ving scowled. He carefully climbed in and they pushed off from the beach. The small outboards started easily, and the four-man team headed upriver.

UBANGI RIVER – Day Four - 0600 hours

They had been traveling upriver through rough water for about eight hours with no major incidents when they hit the biggest section of rapids they had seen. Large boulders stuck up out of the whitewater everywhere, creating narrow channels and swirling currents.

The two boats had remained fairly close together up until then, but the faster current and tricky navigation now forced them several hundred yards apart. Pete and Jared's boat was farthest upstream.

Brad and Ving's boat was sitting deeper in the water because Ving was so heavy, and that became a problem when they entered the rapids. They started taking more water over the gunnels than they could bail out.

Brad yelled at Ving, "Bail faster." Just when they thought they were doomed to sink, they cleared the first rapids and entered a section of calmer water.

The current was still extremely fast in the smoother water, except for an occasional eddy near the riverbank. The guide headed toward the nearest eddy hoping to have time to clear all the water out of the boat.

Ving felt he was sitting too far back in the boat and tried to move a couple of feet forward. Just as he was wiggling his rear end into a comfortable sitting position, a monstrous hippo exploded out of the murky water, surprising the hell out of him.

The giant hippopotamus's head struck the pirogue broadside with immense force, throwing Ving head first into the foul water of the river. He surfaced next to the boat with his big eyes nearly popping out of his head as he yelled, "Shit!" He spluttered and thrashed in the water as Brad quickly reached out to grab Ving's arm and pull him back into the boat.

The Ubangi River current was incredibly strong, and Ving's two hundred and sixty pounds of muscle acted like a sea anchor. The hippo circled the pirogue to get at the infuriating human, which was a fortunate thing for Ving. If the brute had ignored the long wooden boat and surged forward Ving would have been a dead man. Brad knew that hippos killed more people in Africa every year than all the other animals combined, and he was desperately afraid for his friend's life.

For the first time in their twenty-year friendship Brad saw a look of unreasoning fear in Ving's eyes. He reached out to grab him with both hands and pulled with every ounce of strength he had while trying to maintain his balance and not tip over the slim pirogue.

Their river guide was trying to maneuver the pirogue closer to Ving, doing his best to stay between Ving and the raging hippo, but the current was against him. Just as Brad made headway, the current pitched their boat sideways and Brad had to release his friend or be dragged into the water.

The river dragged Ving downstream, and the hippo went after him, moving with astonishing speed through the current. Splashes near the riverbanks alerted Brad, and he glanced up to see the long, sinister forms of several crocodiles slipping into the river . . . they sensed a free meal.

"Oh fuck," Brad yelled. The absurdity of their situation struck him even as his body reacted quickly to take control of the chaos. There was no way, after years of serving together on dangerous military missions all over the globe, that he would let a hippo do Ving in. Watching in helpless, abject horror as Ving got chewed was simply not his style.

Brad shoved the guide away from the tiller arm of the outboard, slamming it all the way to its farthest position. The pirogue nearly capsized as his quick and violent effort caused it to spin in place, but then it righted itself as Brad aimed the front of the slender boat directly at Ving's bobbing head.

Despite his Marine Corps training, Ving had never been what someone would call a great swimmer. He had taken in a great deal of water and was rapidly losing the ability to keep his head above water. Fortunately for him, the strong current was sweeping them all toward the opposite bank and away from the crocodiles, which lay half submerged in the water, waiting patiently for the angry hippo to leave them a few bits and pieces of the large, dark man. Even crocs were wary of hippos. Unfortunately for Ving, the hippo seemed to be indifferent to the power of the current, and it was making a beeline for the struggling man.

When it caught up to Ving, they were only about twenty feet away from the bank, and Brad did something that astounded the unhappy boat captain; he dove into the water and grabbed Ving from behind. Using the standard lifesaving and rescue technique of throwing his arm across Ving's chest, Brad side stroked strongly toward the shoreline. Even with all the adrenaline pumping through his heart it seemed to take forever before he was close enough to touch the bottom. Ving was screaming expletives and kicking at the head of the surprised hippo with his large booted feet.

Brad tugged Ving up onto the beach just as the angry hippo was swept downstream. Ving was getting up in years. In his prime he would have spotted the bank and made a swim for it with no problem. But at his age, with the river current, the hippos, and everything else going on he had just been trying to stay afloat and close to the boat.

They lay panting on the sand, and it took a moment to realize that the immediate danger had passed. Ving raised his head to look at his friend.

"Are you out of your fucking mind?"

Brad exploded into laughter. He rolled over onto his back and laughed until his sides and belly hurt. Ving did the same. If the crocs had come ashore just then they could have had a real feast.

When the laughter died out, and they were lying weakly beside each other, Brad turned his head to Ving. "You're welcome."

The sardonic remark set them both off again, and the boat captain stared at them as if they were insane while he fended off the inquisitive crocodiles with the long pole he used to propel the pirogue when the water became too shallow to use the outboard.

Both men had missed the adrenaline rush they used to get on high-risk missions. It had been several years since their active service and although they had been in hazardous circumstances together on several bounty hunting jobs, this was the first time since they'd fought together in combat that they'd felt the hopeful presence of the grim reaper.

As they sat up they could just see their guide as he turned the pirogue back downstream and disappeared around the bend. "Where the hell is he going?" Brad asked.

"He's abandoning us . . . hightailin' it back to Bangui," Ving growled.

Brad knew they had to reach their destination quickly if they were to have any chance to save Jessica. But so far it seemed everything was going wrong. Even after several days of carefully devising strategy and making plans, they were stranded on a beach beside the Ubangi River in the middle of the fucking jungle, soaked to the bone, watching helplessly as their supplies, weapons, and everything else disappeared downstream. They were truly screwed. Neither of them wanted to think about the parasites and bacteria they'd just been exposed to or that they were now well and truly defenseless. Brad hoped the shots and pills they had taken before starting the trip would be effective.

Brad shook off the self-pity. "Ving," he said, "we've got to get our shit together. We've turned into a couple of pansy-ass civilians. It's been too long since we've mixed it up with some real bad guys on foreign soil. It's time to kick some serious ass."

Ving said, "I'm with you, brother man. What's next?"

"I wanna talk to the man in charge of this frigging jungle. We gotta find this lunatic Ostrigamo."

Ving smiled. "You mean that wild rebel who's recently risen to power? The one who's in bed with Jessica's father?"

"Yeah, that one. What the hell is Jack thinking and why do you think he forgot to mention that little tidbit to me?" Brad replied.

"Who the hell knows. But I'm willing to bet if we locate him, we'll find out."

What do you think is the quickest way to reach this guy?"

"That's easy enough. We just do something in his territory that he don't like."

"Now there's something I can relate to. Let's do it!"

"I have a feeling that will be easier said than done. We're stuck here on the bank of this fucking river, soakin' wet, lost everything we brought with us, and the only son of a bitch who knew this river just went ridin' down the Ubangi totin' our shit with him," Ving said as he stood up to shake the sand out of his pants.

"Don't worry about that," Brad muttered. "It's time to create a firestorm of feculence. What's Ostrigamo's main source of income?"

"Blood diamonds," Ving said.

Brad stood up. "Okay, fine. Then we go steal some of them. That will surely get this Ostrigamo guy's attention."

"Or it'll get us killed," Ving muttered. Then to Brad he said, "Don't you think that might be the same mistake that Jessica made?"

"Can you think of a better way to find her?"

"No, definitely not." Ving shook his head slowly. "Let's do it. But where the hell do we start?"

"We have to find some of his precious blood diamonds," Brad replied. "That Nuru guy should be able to help us with that."

"It's gonna be a long walk to Mobaye from here," Ving muttered.

"Yeah, but not for us," Brad said as the sound of an outboard motor drifted downstream. "Here come Pete and Jared downstream looking for us. I don't imagine they'd mind us hitching a ride in their boat."

"Yeah right." Ving laughed. "The good news is they loaded the extra weapons and gear in their boat to balance out the weight. We can resupply."

It was just about daybreak when Pete and Jared's pirogue nosed into the beach.

"What the hell happened to you two?" Jared asked, staring at their dripping clothes.

"Ving wanted to play with the hippos," Brad said with a straight face. "I can't take this guy anywhere...."

DIAMOND CITY OF MOBAYE

It was nearly 1000 hours before they reached Mobaye. Ving pulled their guide aside and put his arm around his shoulders. "I trust we won't have the same issue with you that we did with the other guide. Correct?" Ving stepped away and showed the man his gun. "Because we can't afford anymore mishaps. Understood?"

"Yes . . . sir. I will take you where you need to go. Will get you there fast. Fast as possible."

Ving clapped the man on the back a bit too hard. "Good man," he said. "Now let's get back to the pirogues and get this show on the road."

As Ving climbed in the boat, Brad asked, "How'd you manage that? The poor bastard looks terrified."

"I told him I'd become good friends with the hippo. Then I told him the hippo promised to eat him if he came back downriver without me."

According to Carson, Nuru owned a trading post near the river and could nearly always be found there. The place served primarily as a front for his black-market dealings. Brad was eager to question him, both about Jessica and Ostrigamo.

They walked up to one of the small docks at the back of the shallow slough where they'd put ashore and asked a tired looking laborer where they might find Nuru, but the man didn't understand English. Brad tried again in French, which was sort of the second language of the CAR because of its earlier status as a French colony, but the man either truly didn't understand or was waiting for Brad to cross his palm with silver. Sighing, Brad reached into his pocket and drew out a silver dollar he carried as a good luck piece. He had a pocket full of U.S. currency, but he didn't know if it had any value in this remote village in the middle of the jungle.

"Nuru," he said slowly, handing the man the coin. The man gradually lifted the silver coin to his mouth and bit into it, hard. He took it out of his mouth and stared at the dent his tooth had made, then looked back at Brad. "Nuru," Brad said again. "Where . . . Nuru?" He sounded like he was talking to a simpleton.

The man smiled. "I presume you are referring to the esteemed proprietor of our local emporium of various articles of clothing and gastronomical delights. If memory serves me, his domicile is attached to the rear of his establishment and I rather think that at this time of day he will be in either one or the other. By the way—" he flashed a broad grin at an astonished Brad "—I would have been perfectly satisfied with one of those instead of this pretty silver coin." He held out the hand with the silver coin and used his other callused hand to point at a hundred-dollar bill peeking out of Brad's pocket, dragged out by Brad's effort to find the coin. The man looked expectantly at Brad, still holding out the silver coin.

Ving howled with laughter. "Pay the man, Brad! That'll teach you to make assumptions." The grinning laborer sounded as if he'd been educated at Harvard.

"Smart ass," Brad muttered to his friend as he handed the laborer the money. The laborer took the hundred and pocketed the silver dollar as well, which sent Ving off into another laughing fit.

"Let's go," Brad snarled, stalking off in the direction the laborer had indicated. "Bring the damned gear."

Mobaye appeared to be a small town. From the river Brad saw it only stretched out a short distance in each direction. A few old buildings scattered here and there, some dwellings of whitewashed concrete block and corrugated roofs and what seemed to be a small airfield at the other end of the town, inland from the river's edge.

As they walked along the edge of the slough, they came abreast of a small building that looked like some kind of restaurant, though there was no sign, not even a screen door over the entrance, but the smell of fresh-cooked bacon wafted through the air.

"That's makin' me hungry," Ving said.

"Get your mind off that pot belly of yours, Ving. Let's find Nuru first." Brad smiled. "You can indulge your bacon fetish later!"

"It's probably long pig anyway, Ving." Pete chuckled. Ving made a face. Long pig was what the more backwards Congolese called human flesh when it was on the menu for supper.

They approached the long, low concrete block building the laborer had pointed to, and the word

'Nuru' was painted over the open doorway on top of a thin skim coat of whitewash in what looked like a child's writing. From the description they got from Carson, they learned that Nuru was a small black man with a bald head and beady little reptilian eyes. "Kind of like a snake," was the description Carson had given.

Uncertain of what they might encounter, Brad muttered, "Let's go in weapons ready."

"Sounds good," Ving growled.

Brad entered first, followed immediately by Ving and the others. There was only one man in the building. "You must be Nuru."

"I am," he replied calmly. "Who might you be?"

"I'm here looking for someone, and I was told you might be able to help me locate her."

"Aaaah, you must be referring to the white woman. You know most people who travel through here are only looking for diamonds," Nuru said easily.

"That's what my cousin Jessica was looking for," Brad replied. "But why the hell would anyone search for a diamond mine in a place already notorious for the blood diamond trade?"

Nuru smiled. "Your cousin is a very smart woman. You see, our diamonds are mined by placer or alluvial mining. There were no glaciers here, so the diamonds are close to the surface. In river sand vast numbers of workers sift through the sand by hand. We call them diamond-diggers.

"Artisanal diamond mining is used when there is a massive, low-cost workforce at hand and requires no expensive equipment. That type of mining is ideal when everything is controlled by an oppressive government or a rebel force. It takes lots of time and manpower to be profitable. As you might say, it's like looking for needles in haystacks.

The needles are there, you just need to have enough laborers looking for them.

"Your cousin Jessica was searching for the source of those diamonds. Local legends tell of an open diamond pit in a large cave discovered by Henry Morton Stanley many years ago. The legend says that the cave is the source from which years of heavy rains and storms have swept the diamonds into the local river system."

"If the cave was discovered years ago, why has no one mined it yet?"

"Ahh. That is an intelligent question. I see Jessica is not the only smart one. Lore says Henry Morton Stanley drew a map to the cave, but never told anyone what he did with it. The map and the diamonds were lost once again."

"How convenient," Brad muttered.

"If one did find such a rare mine as this, an individual could scoop up more diamonds in a single afternoon than an entire workforce might find in weeks, maybe months, of sifting river sand.

"That is what your cousin Jessica has been looking for. I can tell you right now that the rebels know why she is here. They allowed her to search around here quite freely, planning on stealing anything she might actually find. The trick would be finding the cave and then getting out of here alive with the diamonds."

"Do you think she found it?"

"I don't know," replied Nuru. "I heard that she ran into trouble near the Kimberlite Hills at the Kotto River."

"What about the others who were traveling with her?"

"I don't know anything about anyone else."

"Okay. What kind of trouble did she get into?"

"I heard she had a run-in with Ostrigamo."

"The Séléka leader? That Ostrigamo?"

"The very one."

"Where can I find this Ostrigamo?"

"Usually where you least expect him," Nuru said. "He's known for moving around a lot and routinely comes by here several times a week. He normally arrives at the airfield in a small military transport, a Caribou I think you'd call it."

"Where does he keep his diamonds?"

"I'm sure I have no idea, I'm just a poor merchant." Nuru laughed. "All I can tell you is that most of the diamonds found in this part of the country get shipped out of here through the Mobaye airport. The only planes the rebels don't shoot down are the small military transport planes they have seized for their own use. They basically control the airspace around here, and the only thing that flies in or out are the rebels and their diamonds."

Brad had given the wiry little storekeeper several of the wadded up hundred-dollar bills from his pocket, and even though they were still damp, Nuru had accepted them as his due. As they left Nuru's trading post, Brad's intuition told him that he had finally gotten a valid lead on where he might find Jessica, and, incidentally, where they might find Ostrigamo's diamonds.

"Okay, let's go get Ving some bacon for his breakfast and make plans," Brad told his team. "We need to check out the airport for any sign of Ostrigamo and also break out the map and GPS to plan a route to the Kotto River. Pete and Jared, get your breakfast to go and head over to the airstrip as quick as you can. Keep under cover and keep your eyes peeled. Nuru says Ostrigamo comes through there several times a week and I don't want to miss him. Let me know if you see any sign of him."

Ving was already halfway to the eating establishment they had passed earlier. "Hurry up, I'm starving," he called over his shoulder as he raced toward the smell of frying bacon.

CLOSING IN ON HER – Day Four - 1130 hours

They entered the restaurant beneath a small awning which covered the porch at the front door. There were few tables inside, and they appeared to be occupied by locals. Brad decided that either the place was really popular or this tiny town of 3,000 souls had a limited choice of eating establishments.

Pete and Jared went ahead and ordered fried egg sandwiches and coffee to go from the wizened Congolese behind the crude wooden counter while Brad and Ving waited patiently for a table to open up. Pete and Jared were out the door with their takeout order and headed for the airstrip to hunker down and keep a lookout for any sign of Ostrigamo, before Brad and Jared were able to grab a table.

Conversation had come to a complete halt when the four men had entered, and it wasn't long before the customers started finishing up their meals and leaving. The sole waitress, a pretty, young girl in a surprisingly clean dress and apron brought them coffee without asking and asked what they'd like to order.

"Anything with eggs and bacon ... and add a second order of bacon," Ving said, flashing the girl a bright, broad smile.

Brad ordered bacon and eggs as well. The waitress, giving them a nervous smile, went back to give the little woman at the counter their order then hustled back through what passed for a kitchen and out the open back door. Brad watched through the small, dirty window as she collected eggs from the chicken coop.

Brad was sipping coffee and teasing Ving about flirting with the waitress when a white man strode through the door. Brad did a double take and coffee spewed from his lips as he recognized the familiar voice greeting the old woman behind the counter. The woman's face lit up as he walked toward her.

Jack Paul bent over the counter to hug the old woman and they began to chat in French. "What the hell are you doing here, Jack?" Brad asked, standing behind him.

Jack spun around, surprised, but not as much as Brad thought he should have been. Brad's eyes narrowed as his uncle spoke.

"Same as you, Brad, trying to find my daughter," Jack replied. The woman he'd been talking to slipped away and came back a moment later with a coffee for him. "Thanks much," he said to her. Then he turned back to Brad. "Let's sit. There's much I need to update you on."

As they walked to the table where Ving was seated, they heard the sound of more bacon being laid out to sizzle on the massive cast iron wood stove in the kitchen. Soon the waitress came back with their plates, handing Ving one with an enviable mound of bacon stacked on it. There were no biscuits or toast with the meal, there was a small platter of flat bread that looked much like pancakes, which both Brad and Ving knew to be chapati. They looked much like a tortilla but were made with flour instead of cornmeal and were at least twice as thick as a tortilla. Both men knew they were eating enough food to feed a Congolese family for more than a day, but neither had the slightest feelings of guilt. This was not their first trip to the CAR. Their bill would be ten times higher than any Congolese would have had to pay.

"How did you get here so fast, Jack?" Brad asked, his face a blank mask. He took a bite of egg while he waited for his uncle to answer.

"I have certain confidential connections in this part of the world," Jack blustered. Brad saw through the bluster for what it was.

"Cut the crap, Jack. First, it would have been great if you'd shared those connections with me so I could have gotten here faster. Second, you need to tell me why you're here. You asked me to find your daughter. And what? You just decided to pop over to the other side of the world to lend a helping hand. What gives?"

"I wasn't completely honest with you," Jack began. Brad started to say something, but Jack held up his hands to stop him. "It wasn't that I intended to deceive you. I just didn't want to say anything until I knew something one way or the other. But I received information that apparently my daughter has actually found Stanley's legendary diamond mine. That's the good news. The bad news is that this rebel leader, Ostrigamo, has taken her captive."

"We know," Brad said. "We also know that you're somehow involved with him. Care to explain that?"

Jack dismissed him and kept talking. "What's important is that when he grabbed Jessica, he wanted the location of the mine. She gave him that, but he still refused to let her go. Now he wants to meet with me, to sort out some old business dealings we've had in the past. I agreed to meet him about an hour from now at the north end of town at the airstrip hangar. Needless to say, I didn't expect to see you two here."

Bullshit, Brad thought. Brad knew that Jack knew Brad would find Jessica. "So, what's your plan?" Brad asked his uncle.

"I'm confident I can negotiate for her release. Brad, I need you to back off and let me handle this. I appreciate your efforts so far, but I want you to cancel your rescue mission and leave this to me.... Believe me, I'm in a better position to handle this than you are."

Brad had no reason to trust Ostrigamo and he had learned not to believe Jack. Whether his uncle liked it or not, the rescue mission was definitely still on. A sudden thought struck him.

"Have you been keeping track of my progress on this mission, Jack?" A smile spread across Jack's face, but it never reached his eyes. "So that car parked outside my apartment the night before I left was one of your guys?" Jack's politician's smile never faltered. "I want to be at this meeting with Ostrigamo," Brad said angrily.

"Not a good idea. I'm trying to keep this from escalating into a firefight."

"Better a firefight than an execution. You need backup even if you're too stupid to realize it, Jack. Ving and I will go with you."

The smile finally wavered. Jack responded slowly, carefully selecting his words.

"Okay, but I want you guys to hang back. And try to keep the weapons out of sight, would you?"

"Sure thing, Jack."

Brad and Ving finished their coffee, which, in contrast to everything else about the god-forsaken place, was absolutely wonderful, before walking outside and climbing into Jack's vehicle, a brand new and conspicuously clean Jeep, for a ride to the airstrip.

"I'm fortunate that my business associate had this in his garage last night," Jack said conversationally as he sped off toward the grass airstrip. "Somebody broke into my salvage yard last night outside Bangui and stole one of our better delivery trucks."

"Imagine that!" Brad said.

"Yeah, people will steal just about anything that isn't nailed down these days," Ving said. "It's a cryin' damned shame!"

They spotted the incoming small military transport, a C-7A Caribou, just as Nuru had said, as they approached the primitive grass airstrip. As they pulled up behind the main hangar, the transport aircraft touched down on the single runway and began to rumble slowly toward the hangar.

"That has to be Ostrigamo," Jack said. The road to the airstrip passed behind the main hangar before circling around to the front entrance.

"Just drop us off back here, Jack." Relieved, Jack quickly stopped the shiny new Jeep.

"You'll thank me later, Brad, you'll see. This will go much smoother and easier if Ostrigamo doesn't have to talk in front of strangers."

Jack drove away as soon as they were out of the Jeep, hurrying away and not looking back, making his way around to the front of the hangar just as the small transport braked to a full stop.

Brad and Ving exchanged a knowing glance and moved quickly toward the tiny, almost invisible rear access door to the hangar. As they ran, both men checked the belted boxes of ammunition suspended from the sides of the heavy M4A1s that Ving had scared up back in Texas. By longstanding habit, Brad's was set on single fire while Ving's was set for fully automatic. "Pete and Jared should be hiding nearby," Brad whispered.

They entered quietly through the back door. They instinctively spread out, seeking the optimum vantage points from which to observe the meeting. The large hangar seemed clear of personnel except for a small office near the front. There were two guards in M23 uniforms. Both looked as if the noise of the landing aircraft had just awakened them.

As Jack climbed out of the Jeep, the aircraft stopped just a hundred feet away. When the door finally opened, the man Brad assumed was Ostrigamo exited with a small detachment of six men armed with AK47s, all wearing the same camouflaged uniforms as the guards inside.

Jack Paul was nervous as hell. He'd had many business dealings with Ostrigamo over the past couple years, but he'd never met the man face-to-face. Ostrigamo was reputed to have a legendary temper, and Jack knew for a fact that he was no one's fool.

Brad mentally reviewed what he had read about the man in the official Intelligence reports Ving had gathered before the mission. Ostrigamo was one of the founding members of the Séléka Alliance. He was twenty-three years old, about six feet tall, so black that his skin, like Ving's, appeared to be almost blue. He was just so damn ugly. He'd grown up as an orphan living on the streets of Bangui and fighting with the other beggars for scraps of food from the refuse piles of the city.

He was rumored to be mentally unbalanced, fierce, and extremely violent . . . but also known to be resourceful and highly intelligent. Brad realized he was a formidable opponent.

Ostrigamo joined the Democratic Front of the Central African People, an anti-government militia, at the tender age of fourteen. Instinctively he knew that was the only way to get off the streets. He craved power and fame, and he learned that money was power. He also understood that gaining control over a large slice of the blood diamond market would increase his fortune enough to buy his way into power and eventually become the supreme leader of the Central African Republic.

His weaknesses were greed, ego, and a massive case of overconfidence. He wore green and brown military camouflage fatigues and a *tagelmust,* or turban, with a face veil to block the dust and sun. With two ammo belts hanging over his shoulders and a rifle in his hands, he looked as if he had come to fight.

"Where's my daughter?" Jack shouted with no preamble.

Ostrigamo approached Jack slowly. "Relax, Jack, she's somewhere safe. Let's talk a little business before we address the matter of your daughter."

"What do you want?"

"Not a lot, Jack, I'm a reasonable man. I want to modify our original business agreement. I need a bigger percentage of our ongoing trade. I have expenses."

"Why do you even care? What the hell does it matter? Jessica handed you that diamond mine on a platinum platter!"

"Like I said, Jack, I have expenses. I also happen to have a very great need for capital. I have to be concerned about all of my income sources."

"I'm not giving you a damned thing until I see that Jessica is safe."

"Not a good answer, Jack." Ostrigamo's face contorted into an expression of fury. "Perhaps it would be easier if I just killed you right now for your rudeness. Do you have any idea how far away from any kind of help you are right now, white man?" The lunatic side of his personality gleamed in his eyes, and his fingers tightened on the stock of his rifle.

Two of Ostrigamo's men quickly raised their weapons and aimed them at Jack. They had seen Ostrigamo like this before, and they wanted to make damned sure that if their leader got angry and fired on this money man they could honestly say they shot him too. Failure to back up Ostrigamo's actions, no matter how outrageous, was a death sentence.

Jack panicked and ran toward the rear of the hangar where he thought Brad and Ving were hiding.

Brad had no time to consider his options. Jack had proven to be an unworthy asshole, but he was still family. Just as Ostrigamo's men were about kill Jack, Brad and Ving fired almost simultaneously.

Ostrigamo and the four guards he had left were promptly joined by the two rebels from the guard office. The blood-splattered remains of the two who had aimed at Jack were sprawled out on the concrete floor of the hangar. Now Brad's team was outnumbered seven to two . . . Jack didn't count; he was terrified and worthless.

Brad and Ving were able to take out two more of Ostrigamo's men before they had a chance to scramble for cover behind some pallets of cargo near the hangar entrance. The rebels and Ostrigamo were firing nonstop and seemed to have an unlimited supply of ammo.

Uncle Jack somehow found cover along the inside wall of the hangar about halfway back. He was slowly making his way toward Brad.

Severely outgunned, Brad's instincts told him to pull back at the first opportunity and find a battleground of his own choosing, somewhere that would give him an advantage over Ostrigamo's superior numbers, but he refused to leave without Jack.

Ving was holding his own, but he knew that Brad would be making a quick exit as soon as Jack reached him. Ostrigamo loudly ordered one of his men to circle around the outside of the hangar and seal off the rear exit. It was clear that he planned to finish them off in crossfire.

By the time Jack reached Brad, Ostrigamo's soldier had already secured the sole rear exit from the hangar. He started firing into the hangar at Ving from behind.

"We're trapped!" Ving shouted to Brad. Without hesitation Brad swung the barrel of his weapon away from a surprised Ostrigamo and aimed directly at the transport parked outside. Ostrigamo screamed at him as Brad placed three well-aimed shots into the fuel tank of the aircraft. With a roar, it exploded into a massive ball of fire. The blast knocked Ostrigamo to the ground even as Ving took out another rebel, but the odds were still stacked against them.

Brad had a bad feeling about this pitched battle, it hadn't been part of the plan and he wasn't sure they were going to get out of it alive. He handed the M45 MEUSOC pistol he had been awarded on his separation from the Corps to a surprised Jack. "Here, use this!" he shouted. "Keep shooting until you run out of ammo." The rebels were advancing slowly through the stacks of cargo crates. The three of them were pinned down, beset from the front and the rear.... There was nowhere to go.

Suddenly, the sound of gunfire from outside the hangar froze all of them for a second. The rebels at the front of the hangar halted their advance and turned to see where the shots were coming from.

Brad turned and tried to pull back but saw the soldier at the backdoor standing up to take a shot at him. Brad flung his body toward the concrete floor, hitting it hard and waiting for the bullet to strike him.

Just at that moment a heavier caliber shot rang out and the rebel's head exploded in a shower of blood that almost reached Brad's outstretched hands. Brad, Ving, and Jack sprang up and rushed for the open doorway, ignoring the shots coming from behind them.

The rebels unleashed a torrent of gunfire as the three of them fled out the backdoor, and Brad felt bullets tug at his pant leg. He had no idea if he'd been hit, and he was damned if he'd stop to look.

Immediately as they cleared the hangar they saw Pete and Jared. It was Jared's sniper shot that had taken out the soldier at the back of the hangar. Ving turned, flung himself to the ground, and began to rake the back wall of the hangar with automatic fire.

Jared and Pete had seen the small plane land, and then heard the gunfire and the explosion of the plane that occurred almost immediately afterward. There was no doubt that signaled trouble for Brad and Ving; so they busted guts running all the way from where they had taken cover earlier near a smaller hangar at the far end of the airstrip.

"Nice shot," Brad said to Jared. "I should have known it was you. Glad you could make it," he gasped as he checked his legs for wounds. No one had to explain to him that sometimes a round could hit you so hard you didn't really feel it till later. He'd had that experience in Fallujah.

"I hate it when a party starts before I can get there," Jared quipped.

Brad, not finding any damage to himself other than three holes in his trousers' legs where the AK-47 rounds had passed through them, swiftly checked everyone's ammo status.

As they regrouped, Brad gave the order to retake the hangar.

"Keep Ostrigamo alive," he shouted. "We need him to find Jessica. He's got her, I heard him tell Jack he did."

Jack, red-faced and gripping the .45 tightly, asked if Brad had any other magazines for the weapon. Brad fumbled at his belt and removed two more loaded magazines from a pouch. "That's all I've got. If it's any consolation to you, there's a river guide back in Badokwah that has three boxes of cartridges for it in a bag in his pirogue!"

The five of them spread out and rushed the hangar at Brad's command, Ving firing three round bursts from his rifle.

Ostrigamo had survived the gunfight although most of his men were down. He decided to make a run for it. He only liked to fight when he had a distinct advantage and, like Brad, disliked bringing his enemy to bay on a battlefield not of his own choosing. Since his plane had been destroyed, he climbed behind the wheel of Jack's Jeep, screaming at his guards to pile in. With a grinding of gears and a fantail of dirt spitting out from beneath the back wheels, the Jeep sped out of town in a hasty retreat.

TRACK DOWN – Day Four - 1300 hours

"Now you've done it," Jack said angrily, stamping his feet and kicking at the dusty grass of the airstrip like a child throwing a tantrum. "You've sealed Jessica's fate. Any chance we had of buying her freedom is gone."

"Not true," replied Brad calmly, his insides churning as he came down from his battle lust. "Jessica is valuable merchandise to him, and Ostrigamo is too greedy to pass up the opportunity to use her for leverage."

"So what do we do now?" Jack asked.

"First, we gotta get us a ride."

"But we're not even sure where they're headed...."

"Not to worry. I have a plan."

"You mind sharing?"

"He's heading back to his base camp for reinforcements and to restock his ammo. He likes much better odds and he'll want to regain tactical advantage before he confronts us again."

"So how do we find him?"

"We track him down. I planted a GPS tracking device on your Jeep this morning after we left the restaurant. Now all we gotta do is track him back to his base camp. That's probably where he's holding Jessica."

"Why," Jack asked. "You had no way of knowing Ostrigamo would take my vehicle."

"True. But I sure as shit thought you'd try to ditch us."

Jack's voice cracked as he spoke. "I flew almost 8,000 miles to get to my daughter. My only concern is Jessie."

Brad shook his head. He was starting to believe the duplicitous bastard actually did care about his daughter.

"Ving, check the tracker. Which way are they headed?" Brad asked.

"Through the jungle toward the Kotto River," Ving answered.

"Pete, take Jared and snatch us up a vehicle."

"Roger that!" Pete replied. "Let's go, Jared."

It only took twenty minutes for Pete and Jared to return with both a Jeep and a four-wheel drive pickup, but neither vehicle looked very reliable.

"Okay, load up," Brad commanded. "We're burning daylight." He jumped in to drive the old Jeep while Ving rode shotgun. Jack sat quietly in the backseat. Pete and Jared took the pickup. They headed toward the far side of the airstrip where they'd seen Ostrigamo roaring away in Jack's new Jeep.

They took the same dirt road, which quickly wound its way into the jungle. The road was extremely rough and muddy, which made for very slow going. Ving kept his eyes on the tracking unit.

After half an hour Ving said, "They've stopped about six miles ahead. We're closing in on them."

"Jack, how much gas was in that Jeep of yours?" Brad asked.

"It had over half a tank. But this road is a little rougher than even the Jeep was designed for. They could easily have had a mechanical breakdown," Jack replied.

"We're gonna find out soon enough."

Twenty minutes later, they pulled up carefully behind Jack's Jeep, looking for any sign of Ostrigamo or his soldiers. It was instantly apparent why Ostrigamo had stopped there.

"Ain't no more road," Ving grunted. What had been a rough dirt road had morphed into a narrow hiking trail through the jungle, far too narrow for any vehicle.

"Well, now we're screwed," Jack said. "The GPS tracker is still in the Jeep."

"Oh, ye of little faith!" Brad said, chuckling. "We'll just track them down the old-fashioned way." Brad and his team were all trained and experienced trackers.

"Ving, you lead," Brad commanded. "Pete, you and Jared grab what gear we've got left and bring up the rear. Jack, try to keep up." As they made their way up the trail the jungle seemed to close in around them. The heat and humidity were stifling, and they were still moving slowly on foot.

"Let's pick up the pace a little, Ving," Brad barked.

"I was just thinking," Ving responded, "this guy Ostrigamo is just the kind to set up an ambush. And your uncle Jack can barely keep up at this pace."

"Good points. But if it starts to rain in this jungle these tracks are gonna be all but impossible to follow." Brad passed Ving to take the lead. "Jared, keep Jack on pace," he called to the back.

The trail wound its way gradually upwards into the foothills. The jungle was so thick that visibility was down to two or three meters. They trekked on for perhaps another two hours, going deeper into the jungle.

Brad came around a bend in the trail and came to a complete stop, his clenched fist in the air a signal for the others to stop. There was a small clearing in front of him and standing in the center of it was an enormous bull elephant. Coming face-to-face with an elephant was enough of a shock, but what Brad saw sitting on the neck of the beast left him thunderstruck.

"I'm not fuckin' believing this," he muttered.

"What's up, brother, what is it?" Ving asked from behind him.

"It's a fuckin' pygmy riding an elephant," Brad said dryly.

"Jesus Christ, Brad, this ain't no time for jok—"

Ving's mouth dropped as he looked up at the gray hulk of a beast with two giant curved ivory tusks sticking out of its face and a tiny, brown man with a bone through his nose sitting astride its wide neck. One of the elephant's large floppy ears twitched as it eyed the puny humans standing before it.

Several more elephants emerged from the jungle, all ridden by the strange pygmies. The five-man patrol was surrounded.

Ving glanced up into the trees around them and counted at least thirty more pygmies scattered along the broad limbs before he stopped counting. They were positioned strategically in almost every large tree and they seemed to have appeared out of nowhere.

Any disadvantage they might have had because of their small stature was more than made up for in their numbers and their elevation, not to mention the herd of elephants their 'cavalry' was riding. Small men, barely four feet tall, they were armed with blowguns or bows, and all were aimed at Brad and his men.

"No sudden moves," Brad said quietly, primarily for Jack's benefit. The original bull elephant Brad had seen when he rounded the bend in the road, the one with the guy who appeared to be the leader on his back, took three slow, ponderous steps forward. The pygmy held out his hands, palms up, apparently to show that he bore no weapon. It appeared that he wanted to talk. Brad took a couple of slow steps forward to meet him.

"You are strangers in our jungle," the pygmy said, his English slow, labored, and heavily accented. His face was dead solemn.

"Yes," Brad replied. "We mean you no harm."

"Why are you here?"

"I am searching for a woman, a woman of my blood. We are following a man named Ostrigamo and his soldiers."

"Ostrigamo is known to me. He is a bad man. You hunt these men?"

"Yes," Brad replied.

"After you find this woman, you will leave our forest?" the pygmy leader asked.

"Yes, I promise. As soon as we find her."

"Good luck on your hunt," the pygmy replied. He then turned his elephant and disappeared into the jungle.

They watched as the other elephants turned and marched after the largest one and the strange little man who was their leader. When Ving looked back up into the trees, there was nothing there but the leaves that grew there. He shivered.

"What the hell?" Ving said as he finally let out his breath.

"Those men are of the Mbuti tribe," said Jack, "also known as the forest people, and they're sworn enemies of the Séléka. The Mbuti have lived in this jungle for hundreds of years. They're the oldest indigenous people in this part of Africa."

"How do you know so much about them?" Ving asked.

"It's always wise to know the enemy of your enemy," Jack replied. "The Mbuti live off the land. Rebels have been destroying their rivers with widespread diamond mining. The rebels have also enslaved many of the pygmies to work as diamond diggers. That's led to an ongoing confrontation between the two. The Mbuti consider this ancient rainforest their ancestral homeland and the Séléka as trespassers and rightly so. They've lived here since the Stone Age."

"That seems like an unfair match," said Ving. "The Séléka with AK-47s and the pygmies with blowguns and bows."

"The Mbuti's knowledge of the terrain, their stealth in the jungle, and the sheer power of those elephants have made them more than a worthy opponent for the rebels. On top of that, the elephants scare the hell out of the Séléka, who believe the pygmies possess great magic. You wouldn't believe how accurate they are with those damned blowguns and their poison darts. The Séléka absolutely refuse to move out here in the darkness. The Mbuti sneak up on them and shoot those poison darts from high in the trees. Mbuti are flatly invisible at night, and, trust me, around here, they own it."

"Good to know," Brad said. "Now, let's get going, I want to narrow the gap with Ostrigamo before dark." Jack moaned. He'd been hoping for more time to catch his breath.

"Ving, how much farther to the Kotto River?" Brad asked.

Ving checked his GPS coordinates against the topographical map he'd stored in a waterproof bag inside the now much lighter rucksack he carried on his back. "It's three more miles to the river, but then this trail turns and runs upriver to the Kimberlite Hills that Nuru told us about."

"Let's try to make it to the river where we can camp for the night," Brad said. He didn't want to stop. Jessica was close, he could sense her. He had no choice but to stop, though. Jack was at the end of his strength, and the team wouldn't do Jessica any good if they were too tired to fight. There was no doubt in Brad's mind that Ostrigamo was going to fight, no doubt at all.

CONFRONTATION – Day Five – 0500 hours

Ving woke everyone before the crack of dawn.

"It's still dark out," Jack grumbled.

"We leave in ten minutes," Brad said quietly. The insects were horrible; they'd kept the team from getting any real rest.

As they left their riverside camp Brad took the lead. The tracks of Ostrigamo and his men were getting harder to follow along the riverbank and there were more side trails and footprints to examine. It was slowing them down but they only had about four miles to go before they reached the Kimberlite Hills. Brad hoped that might be where Ostrigamo's camp was located. He had wanted to push on last night, but they'd been exhausted and traveling in the dark through this jungle was just too damned dangerous.

As they traveled upriver they came to a smaller tributary joining the Kotto from their left. It was fifteen feet across, but fast and deep. Brad looked for a good place to cross.

Ving checked his GPS and his map once more. "This is Gouda Creek." Roughly fifty yards up the Gouda they could see the creek coming over the ridge and dropping in a hundred-foot waterfall. Brad was trying to find the spot where Ostrigamo and his men must have crossed, but it wasn't easy.

"Do you think they climbed the ridge and crossed above the falls?" Jared asked.

"Not sure," said Brad. He turned and followed a well-worn path along the Gouda toward the falls. His head down looking for signs of passage, Brad almost missed the crossover point. There was a narrow gap over the creek where large boulders jutted out from both sides. It was fifty feet from the base of the falls, and the rocks were wet and slippery as hell. The gap appeared to be nearly eight feet across; Brad figured they could all jump it, even Jack. A misstep would see the jumper drop twenty feet into the fast rushing water of the creek below.

"I'll go first," Brad said as he handed his rifle and rucksack to Ving. He backed up a few steps and took a run at it. He cleared the distance easily.

"Throw some of the gear over," he shouted above the roar of the falls. Pete and Jared began tossing gear to him. Pete backed up a few steps and made a quick run. He cleared the gap by several feet and helped Brad catch the rest of the gear.

"Send Jack over next!"

Jack looked at the gap dubiously. Clearly nervous, he was the oldest and least physically fit of the group. "Fuck it," he muttered. He backed away, twice as far as the others had to get a longer run at it. But he backed into the hanging branches of the rainforest without looking, and suddenly he was staring into the flat, black eyes of a huge green snake nearly nine feet long. It was dangling just inches from his head. He froze. "Snake!" he whimpered in a tiny voice.

"Don't move," Ving said, approaching Jack cautiously with Jared close behind.

"Is it poisonous?" Jack asked softly as the fear took him. He was shivering.

"It's a mamba, a Jameson's Mamba to be more precise," Ving said as nonchalantly as he could manage. "Powerful neurotoxin. If he bites you'll be dead in less than thirty minutes, so shut up and stay the fuck still."

The snake had been startled by Jack's intrusion into its domain and was hissing loudly. It raised its narrow, elongated head; its round pupils locked on Jack. It flattened its neck. It was preparing to strike and Ving knew it, though he couldn't think of a damned thing he might do to stop it. Two shots went off right beside his ear, and Ving immediately clapped his hands over his ears. He turned and saw Jared standing beside him, an M45 pistol with its barrel smoking held loosely in his hand. The long, yellow-green snake dropped, slithered over Jack's shoulder, and fell dead at his feet. Jack felt light-headed as if he were about to pass out. He stumbled out of the overhanging branches and sat on a large boulder near the creek.

Ving seemed surprised at how fast Jared had reacted to the threat, but at the same time he was irate. Guns going off in his ear tended to piss him off and he glared at the younger man.

"You looked like you were freaking out," Jared said with a loud laugh.

"What the hell's going on over there?" Brad yelled.

"Your uncle Jack just had an up-close and personal encounter with a Jameson's Mamba," Ving yelled back. "It's okay though, I'm only gonna be deaf in one ear!"

"Okay guys, get the hell over here and let's get going. We're wasting time."

As they moved farther up the trail, they reached a clearing where it appeared the rebels had spent the night. Brad could tell from the freshness of the tracks leaving the campsite that they were gaining ground.

Pete found evidence that they were in one hell of a hurry. "I don't know what these guys are eating, but I'm telling you right now I'll starve before I let any of it pass my lips!" He was holding his nose and walking out of the foliage, his eyes locked on the ground as if he were looking for something. "They didn't even stop to dig a hole, man. Whoever that was just dumped his load right on the ground and kept going." He looked up at Brad. "And they're nasty too. No sign of toilet paper, not even a crumpled up leaf with crap on it." He reached around and tugged at the seat of his own pants, even though he was a fastidious man who never even walked around his own hometown without a packet or two of military ration toilet paper in his pocket. "Nasty fuckers!"

The trail continued along the river, and there was a string of hills parallel to the river approximately a half mile to the left. Their topographical map showed that these were the Kimberlite Hills. The ridge of hills appeared to gradually draw closer to the river as they continued north.

As they advanced, the trail climbed higher and higher above the water as it got squeezed between the river and the encroaching hills. There were occasional breaks in the ridgeline where narrow, deep canyons had been carved out by small tributaries that emptied into the Kotto River.

The trail got rough as they repeatedly dropped to cross these narrow side canyons and then clambered up the other side to a point high above the water level. A series of caves began to appear near the base of the hills.

"These volcanic hills are riddled with caves," Jack explained. "For every one we can see there are probably ten more hidden deep in the jungle. Most of them are very shallow, but a few of them are extremely deep. Due to the high concentration of kimberlite in the caves, the potential for diamonds is very promising. The caves you can see from the trail have been searched many times over the years. It's the caves hidden deep in the rainforest that are the source of the ancient legends."

Brad and Ving, tightly focused on tracking Ostrigamo and his men, had virtually tuned Jack out.

As they negotiated a large bend in the trail they viewed a smaller river joining the Kotto down in the valley below. It was larger than any of the creeks they had encountered so far. Brad had no idea how they were going to cross it.

Ving stopped and checked his map. "This is the Bongou River, the largest tributary of the Kotto."

"Let's get down there and check it out," Brad murmured. "We're closing in on these guys."

As they reached the bottom of the small valley where the Bongou and the Kotto merged, they discovered two small pirogues that had been dragged up on the beach.

"Looks like they were left here by the locals for crossing the river," said Jared.

"Yes, but the rebel tracks follow the smaller trail up this side of the Bongou," Brad observed. "We gotta keep moving."

Jared did a little mental muttering. He wasn't a wuss, but except for the snake and the little half-assed fracas at the airfield this mission had just been plain uncomfortable. Not that he really minded; Brad and Ving were both super guys and he owed them big time, but that didn't keep him from being bored.

The jungle became denser along the Bongou and visibility became very limited. After they traveled another two miles the river valley widened, and Brad signaled a halt.

"What's up?" Pete asked from behind.

"The tracks leave the trail here and head straight into the jungle," Brad told him. "We're damned close. Heads up, everybody get ready. Remember to maintain noise discipline!" His voice had dropped to a stage whisper.

"Let's go." They formed into a single file at Brad's hand signal and cautiously made their way into the dense jungle, following the faint tracks of Ostrigamo and his men along an ill-defined game trail. There was no real trail here, just occasional footprints and disturbed vegetation. It would have been impossible to follow for any but the most

142

experienced of trackers, but that was exactly what Brad's team were. All four of them were extremely good at their craft, and Brad was the best of them. He sensed that Jessica was near.

The ground sloped uphill, and he could see what appeared to be a ridgeline up ahead.

Nearly a hundred yards shy of the ridgeline the jungle thinned out considerably and Brad saw a large cave at the base of a vertical rock face. He squatted and spread his arms, indicating that they should form a V. Pete, Jared and Ving spread out roughly fifteen feet apart, and Jack, confused by the hand signals that he did not understand and frustrated by Brad's silence, crept up behind him.

All four Marines could feel the tension. None of them could have explained it to another living soul, but every combat veteran understands the mixture of exultation and abject fear that makes their hearts pound hard enough that they'd think they were going to explode—the feeling of impending contact with the enemy. Ving was to his left, Pete to his right, then Jared to Pete's right. Jack was right on Brad's tail, but there was no time to move him away. The best Brad could hope for was that when the shit hit the fan, Jack would have enough control left to keep him from accidentally shooting Brad in the back. As they crept carefully toward the cave, something went wrong and all hell broke loose.

Gunfire from at least a dozen AK-47s rained down on them and they all scrambled for cover. After about twenty seconds the gunfire stopped and there was an uneasy silence.

"These guys are dug in good," Ving whispered. "They're spread out across the entire base of that cliff, and a few of them are even in the trees. What's our move?"

Before Brad could respond, Ostrigamo appeared at the mouth of the cave, holding Jessica in front of him as a shield. Brad could see the look of terror on Jessica's face and he could see the bastard fondling her left breast as he held a pistol to her temple with his right hand. Ostrigamo was leering like the demonic pervert that he was. A cold feeling of grim determination swelled inside Brad's chest.

"Jack, who are your friends?" Ostrigamo asked loudly. "Tell them to drop their weapons or I will kill your daughter." Jack was frozen in fear, clinging to a tree and unable to speak.

Brad finally responded. "We're just here for the girl. Give her to us and we're outta here."

Ostrigamo backed into the cave, shouting to his men in Bantu and dragging Jessica with him. The soldiers cut loose, firing their weapons indiscriminately. Brad and the others were skilled. None of them had settled for just concealment, they had all sought cover, protection from flying lead. Brad and his men had no choice but to return fire.

Battle drill, pounded into Brad's head as a boot, kicked into overdrive. He waved everyone ahead, weapons blazing in a full frontal assault. The theory of "battle drill" was that when a small unit can't disengage from an enemy in any direction without exposing their backs, the only intelligent thing to do is rush directly at the enemy, making as much noise as possible and putting as much lead into the air as can be managed.

With a little luck the enemy would be too surprised and shocked by the noise and fire, and the speed of the assault, to react effectively, and at least some members of the attacking unit would get behind the enemy lines before the defenders managed to take down the entire unit. Once the enemy's lines had been penetrated, the attackers would be able to mop up the defense, now caught between them.

This time the battle drill didn't work. Brad and the others faced a true wall of lead, and their forward progress was halted. The rebels occupied the high ground and Brad's team was vastly outnumbered.

Jared managed to take out a rebel twenty yards to the right hiding in a tree. Brad returned fire from behind a thick fallen log as he tried to assess the size of Ostrigamo's force. As best he could tell, they were facing a minimum of fifteen men. Bullets streaked over his head and shredded the jungle foliage all around him.

Ving shot a rebel on the ground to the left of the cave entrance. The firefight seemed to rage on forever, and Brad knew his team had to be getting low on ammo. They were outmanned and outgunned, but he wasn't ready to give up.

He was determined to get Jessica, and once more he urged everyone forward. Pete stood up and ran forward five paces then took up a new position behind another fallen log. As soon as he hit the ground he brought fire to bear on the soldiers directly to Brad's twelve o'clock. Then it was

Jared's turn to move up, and as soon as he rose to a kneeling position in order to get his feet under him, Brad saw him go down, his face contorted with pain, his non-firing hand covering his bicep. He glanced at Brad, his eyes filled with pain and shock, but he didn't even call out. Brad scrambled on his belly to reach him. The wound was a "through and through,"—the bullet hat hit nothing solid. There was little damage to the muscle and no bone impact. At that moment Brad knew they had to find a way to fall back. It hurt his very soul, so close to Jessica, but they were badly outnumbered and hopelessly outgunned.

Retreat was not an easy choice for Marines, but they had no other option. There was no way they could help Jessica if they got themselves killed trying to get to her. Brad hated the thought of leaving her behind. "Pull back," he shouted. "Peel!" ordering a diagonal retreat, a tactic that is effective for a small ground unit attempting to withdraw from a confrontation with a much larger force.

148

Brad's earlier full frontal assault had confused and frightened the less experienced M23 troopers. They weren't badly trained, but they had never been faced with anyone who fought with ferocity and courage the way these white men had. Most of their previous battles had been against the Mbuti or the Hutu.

Brad withdrew his team the way he had moved them forward, by leapfrogging one man while the others did their best to provide covering fire. Ostrigamo's men were happy to let them go, even though the action could be fairly compared to letting go of a mamba one had accidentally grabbed by the tail.

Brad finally completed their disengagement when he remembered the hand grenades in his cargo pockets. He tossed two, one after the other in quick succession, and the team moved together in a concerted rush back to the banks of the Bongou River to reassess the situation.

REGROUP – Day Five - 1500 hours

Brad was furious over what he saw as his failure to rescue Jessica.

"Ving, take care of Jared's shoulder," he barked. "Pete, check ammo."

Jack could see that Brad was agitated and tried to stay out of his way, and he was afraid they might have lost their only chance to save Jessica, but it wasn't Brad he blamed. He blamed himself.

"How is Jared?" Brad asked.

"He'll live," Ving replied. "But he needs to take it easy."

"What's our ammo status, Pete?" Brad asked grimly.

"We're down to eighty-five rounds total," Pete said.

He sounded as dismal as Brad felt. With virtually no ammo and facing a superior force, their situation seemed hopeless.

"Do you think that cave they're hiding in is the one full of diamonds that Jess was looking for?" Ving asked.

"That's a strong possibility considering the way they're defending it," Brad replied, "but to tell you the truth, Ving, I couldn't give a shit about the diamonds right now. I just want to get Jessica and get the fuck outta this country."

"So what's our next move?"

"We lost a good bit of our ammo when you decided to go for a swim with that hippo," Brad said.

"You never let a little problem like ammo stop us before," Ving retorted with a grin.

Brad knew Ving was right. There was a solution to every problem. Sometimes finding the solution was a little more difficult, but there was always an answer. He just needed to figure out what it was. He felt better knowing he could count on Ving to remind him that they had survived worse situations.

There was no sound from the direction of Ostrigamo's troops, so Brad patted Ving on the shoulder and walked the few steps down to the river's edge to wash his face and take a few minutes to clear his head. Then, he remembered his Marine Corps training—*"Improvise, adapt, and overcome"*. He kept attacking their situation from different perspectives, searching for alternative solutions. After cooling off some, he had a startling thought, one that should have come to him sooner.

"Wait here, Ving," he called back to his friend, "I'll be back as soon as I can."

"Where the fuck are you going?"

"To get reinforcements!"

Ving wondered if his friend had lost his mind.

Brad had come to the obvious conclusion that, since he was outgunned and outnumbered, his team was doomed. They'd brought enough ordnance to handle a situation like this one; they'd anticipated it and had planned for this contingency. What they hadn't planned for, what they hadn't foreseen, was that damned hippo scaring their boat captain away. Without that extra ordnance, they were in no shape to take on Ostrigamo.

Without the ordnance, Brad needed help, and there was only one source of help that might be possible this deep in the jungle. Ostrigamo hadn't proved to be the apex predator in this primeval hellhole. The Mbuti had.

He wasn't even sure the Mbuti would help, but they were his only option. Brad set out down the trail at a steady lope, but he traveled less than a mile before his internal alarms went off. He stopped, his breathing well under control, and went to one knee. Someone was watching him.

After a brief rest, he moved on, but only made it about another mile down the trail before he came to a stop. He had a feeling he was still being watched. He hadn't actually seen anyone. It was just a feeling in his gut. The jungle was thicker there and visibility was limited. He took a long drink of water from his canteen and then he saw it. It was time to wait.

The colossal elephant emerged from the jungle right in front of him. *How the hell do they do that? How in the hell can you keep a three-and-a-half-ton elephant from making noise when he walks through jungle so thick a man can barely move in it? Maybe these little fuckers really are magic!*

The leader of the Mbuti looked down at him from his perch atop the enormous beast.

"I didn't expect to find you so soon," Brad said.

"We have been following you. My name is Juma," the little man said in his slow and tortured English.

"Why did you follow us?"

"You are a small band. You are hunting a fierce enemy. Your enemy is my enemy. I think you might need my help." Juma then made a circling motion with his arm and a dozen more elephants with Mbuti on their backs emerged from the jungle.

"Yes, we could truly use your help," Brad said, "but what I really need is ammunition for my weapons."

Juma tapped the elephant's shoulder with his staff and the creature knelt down, curling his forelegs beneath him. Effortlessly, Juma slid down off his elephant. "Follow me."

He led Brad on a nearly invisible trail a short way into the jungle where another elephant bearing two very large, heavy-looking crates knelt on the jungle floor. This one had all four legs under him.

Juma gestured regally toward the crates. "These are of little use to us," he said, "but Ostrigamo covets them. He covets them so much that we felt it necessary to relieve him of the burden of guarding them. You are free to take them if they will help you against the crazy man."

Brad recognized the Russian markings on the outside of the crates. One crate had a dozen AK47 rifles and the other held matching ammo.

"No problem," Brad said.

"Ostrigamo and his men are a problem," Juma said, "a problem we would like to see go away and leave us alone. We will help you this one time, so we can bring an end to Ostrigamo," he said sternly, "but then you must leave us."

"No problem," Brad said, echoing his last words. "We will leave as soon as we can." He really was at a loss for words. He heard a rustling in the trees above him, and he followed Juma's disapproving eyes up into the trees. At least fifty Mbuti were looking down on him, one of whom had a sheepish look on his face. He had been the one that made the leaves in the tree rustle. Brad could have sworn the others were smiling.

* * *

It was nearly 1800 hours by the time Brad and the Mbuti made it to the temporary camp. Brad used the short travel time to formulate a new plan of attack using Juma's Mbuti and the weapons.

Thanks to Juma's self-serving generosity, Brad now directed enough of a force to stomp a mudhole in Ostrigamo's ass, literally, but he had to do it such a way as to keep Jessica from harm.

"Holy shit!" Ving exclaimed in awe. Pete, Jared, and Jack just stood, staring at the elephants with their mouths open. Brad understood how they felt. Even though the others had been near the beasts just the day before, they were impressive as hell up close.

"I told you I was bringing reinforcements," Brad said with a wicked grin. He turned and beckoned to Juma to join them as he quickly went over his new plan to rescue Jessica.

The crates were offloaded shortly afterwards, and Juma led his people into the jungle for the night. The old man had appeared to be a little troubled when Brad insisted on waiting until morning to conduct the assault; the Mbuti were extraordinary night fighters. The trait was also part of their mystique, or, as they referred to it, their magic. Convincing the elderly pygmy that Brad and his Recon Marines would provide the necessary magic since Juma had provided adequate weapons and ammunition was one of the most difficult tasks Brad had ever undertaken. Oddly enough, it was Jack who finally convinced the man.

After dark, Brad sent Pete to Ostrigamo's camp to recon their objective and to observe any changes.

THE SHOWDOWN – Day Six

Daybreak came swiftly and Brad was eager to get started. This time they knew their target. "Listen up," he said walking around their makeshift camp, checking everyone. "Let's get a move on. Jack got up and checked his watch. Brad rolled his eyes, wondering why he'd bothered to come at all. He offered no help and in many ways was slowing them down. "Jared." Jared sat up, cradling his arm. "Since you're injured and Jack, you . . . well, since you are not combat trained like the rest of us, the two—"

"Hold up now." Jack puffed out his chest. "I have more life experience than the—"

Brad had had enough of his uncle. If not for Jack's dealings with Ostrigamo, Jessica wouldn't have been in Africa at all, never mind been kidnapped and held.

"Whatever, *Jack*. We don't have time to get in a pissing contest now. You asked *me* for help so shut up, sit down and let me do what I'm trained for."

Brad caught Ving's eye and he smiled. He'd been hearing for years what a righteous pain in the ass Jack was. He thought it was high time someone put him in his place. Near as he could figure, it was long overdue. "Anyway," Brad continued. "As I was saying, since Jared is hurt and Jack isn't helpful, the two of you will circle around and approach from the north, along the top of the cliff face above the cave." He gestured in the direction of the caves. "From there, you will be as safe as can be expected, but you'll still be able to bring firepower to bear on the soldiers Ostrigamo has posted on the outside of the cave."

"Really Brad," Jared said, letting go of his arm. "I'm okay. Take me with you."

Brad approached Jared and put his hand on Jared's good shoulder. "No way. You're more valuable to the team posted by the caves. We need the element of surprise. Having you at half-speed down here isn't going to help any of us." He glared at Jack. "Trust me."

"Okay, I guess you're right. Jack and I will head to the caves. What will the rest of you be doing?"

"You two go around. Pete, Ving and I will take on a direct frontal assault at the cave entrance." He took a breath and prayed. "Let's go." He made eye contact with each man, one by one. "Once we start firing, my chronograph will count down five minutes. When that time is up, we will rush the cave and meet you there. Any questions?" He didn't wait for anyone to speak. There was no time. "Good. See you on the other side."

He led Ving and Pete to the caves. When he could see the guards posted out front, he stopped and turned to his men. "Let's get as close in as we can," Brad whispered as they crawled on their bellies, moving from cover to cover. When he was sure he could fire his weapon and hit the guard, he stopped again. He only had one chance. If he fired at one of Ostrigamo's people and missed, they'd know they were being ambushed and he and his team would be as good as dead. He waved Pete and Ving apart. He readied his weapon, slithered into the jungle floor as deep as he could get and looked through the scope at the unsuspecting soldier. He'd killed before and he would kill again. Never would he kill for as good of a reason as saving Jessica. It never got easier. He was a trained military soldier. He did what he had to, to protect his country and his family. But he never forgot in the end he was still taking a life. Someone's son. Maybe someone's father. He focused as he held the weapon and then initiated the attack by firing the first shot directly into the forehead of the soldier closest to the cave entrance.

The remaining two soldiers startled and in a matter of seconds had their weapons aimed and were firing at Brad, Ving and Pete. But the three had taken cover deep in the earth and the rebels couldn't see who they were firing at. They just knew one of their own was down. Brad and his team inched their way toward the cave, exchanging heavy gunfire with the rebels. Brad kept an eye on his chronograph, and as the sweep second hand ticked toward five minutes, he readied himself to blitz into the cave. He inserted a fresh thirty-round magazine into the magazine well of the AK-47 and took a deep breath. He hoped the cheap Timex Jack had given the Mbuti leader kept good time.

The elephants weren't quiet this time as they thundered out of the jungle. The Mbuti warriors appeared almost magically in the upper tree branches and the air filled with tiny poison darts. Ostrigamo's soldiers began to scream, and they began to die.

Frantic rebels leaped up from covered positions, their terrified eyes wide, their hands slapping futilely at the miniscule darts stuck in their skin. Ving took precise aim at the heads popping up, squeezing off rounds carefully. The AK-47 was nowhere near as accurate as his M4A1, but, as close as he was, it didn't make a great deal of difference. At that range, he could still keep the rounds within a four-inch circle, and that was adequate for head shots. The rebels dropped quickly.

"Right on cue," Ving shouted.

"Cover me!" Brad yelled. He ran for the cave entrance, dodging the marauding elephants busily trampling the fleeing soldiers who had managed to avoid the darts as well as the carefully aimed fire of Ving and Pete.

Jared and Jack fired into the backs of the firing positions of the rebel soldiers, and the whole scene was utter chaos. At that point it was only luck and fate that would determine if Brad were going to make it into the cave alive. Without any formal training, Jack fired blindly, hoping he wasn't going to hit his nephew.

Brad dove inside the cave entrance, crawling behind a large rock. "Jessica," he shouted. The sound of rifle fire echoed in the cave as Ostrigamo and one of his guards opened up on him. Powdered rock and stone chips rained down on Brad. He covered his head with his hands and rolled away from the falling rock. "Jessica!" he yelled again.

"There are only two of them," Jessica yelled. A brief lull in the rifle fire allowed Brad to hear the sound of a hard slap and a muffled cry. He slipped to one side of the rock and got off a shot. The guard dropped, his rifle clattering to the floor of the cave as his eyes rolled up in his head. Brad got a glimpse of Jessica as Ostrigamo knelt over her. Her hands and feet were tied, but she'd ripped out her gag. She was dirty, skinnier than usual and had the wild look of fear in her eyes.

"Dammit," Brad said to no one. The bastard was holding Jessica across his body. The AK was unfamiliar enough that Brad was fearful of taking a chance at a headshot. Even a tiny bit of recoil could screw up his aim and make him hit his cousin. He cursed the fact that his M4A1 was now worthless. If he had had it in his hands at that moment, Ostrigamo would already have been a memory. He waited for a moment for Ostrigamo to move so he could maybe get a clear head shot. But he knew the rebel was too smart for that. Jessica was his shield. His insurance policy.

"It's just you and me now, Ostrigamo." Brad yelled. "Your men are either dead or running for the hills. Let me have Jessica and you can go." That hadn't been his plan. He'd come to Africa to track down and kill his cousin's captor. But now, his only concern was getting Jessica and his team out alive. He couldn't give a damn about Ostrigamo or the diamonds. "You're outnumbered. We've killed most of your men. And we have more ammunition than you." He had no idea if either of those were true. But, he'd learned long ago when he said things with conviction, people believed him.

He gingerly worked his way toward the back of the cave where Ostrigamo and Jessica were half standing. As he moved, he glanced down in amazement. The floor of the cave was littered with rough diamonds, hundreds of them. Maybe thousands.

"I've called for reinforcements," Ostrigamo screamed. "No one is taking my diamonds."

"They're my diamonds," Jessica shouted defiantly, "I found them."

Ostrigamo slapped her in the face and she yelped in pain. "They are mine!" he shouted. "You have no rights to them. You have no right!"

Ving entered the cave, throwing himself to the rough floor a few feet away from Brad. He took up a prone firing position, sighting in on the portion of Ostrigamo's head that was clear of Jessica's. He wasn't confident enough to take the shot; the AK-47 was just not familiar enough to him. He shook his head "no" to Brad and Brad understood his meaning. "I know," Brad said. "Can't risk it." The men had been friends and partners long enough that they understood each other's shorthand.

"You can kill me now," Ostrigamo said. "But the minute your finger pulls the trigger, I'll shoot her." He cocked his gun and pressed the barrel of the weapon to the side of Jessica's head. "If I die, so does she."

Brad didn't know enough about the enemy to know if he were bluffing, and he wasn't about to risk Jessica's life to find out. "We don't need to kill you," he said. "You see how my friend Ving here just appeared out of nowhere with his oh so pretty AK-47?" He followed Ostrigamo's eyes to Ving's weapon. "Well, I got fifty more Vings out there just waiting to come in. We don't have to kill you. We'll just take you into custody. Handsome man like you, you'll love prison. Or at least it'll love you."

Ostrigamo swung his head from side to side, looking around like a caged animal. "Stupid, stupid girl," he said. "If only you hadn't stuck your nose where it doesn't belong." He stamped his foot. "Dammit! Tell me," he pointed at Brad, "why you're here. Is it just to get the girl?"

Brad held up his hands the best he could without letting go of his weapon. "I just want Jessica. You can keep your diamonds. Just give me my cousin."

Ostrigamo glanced behind his shoulder. It was then that it occurred to Brad that he didn't know the caves at all. It was possible that there was a back exit in the labyrinth of tunnels. Brad made eye contact with Ving and Ving shrugged. They were thinking the same thing. They'd trade Ostrigamo's freedom for Jessica's.

"Enough is enough," Brad said to Ostrigamo. "Just give us Jessica."

Accepting the inevitable, Ostrigamo shoved Jessica toward Brad and Ving and she went down on all fours. Then he turned and fled to the back of the cave. Brad thought about firing on him, but there were too many variables. He still wasn't comfortable with the AK-47 and if the bullet ricocheted off the cave walls, one of his own could get killed. It wasn't worth it. His job was to bring Jessica back safely. He didn't care about Ostrigamo or whatever twisted deal Jack had going with the rebel.

Ving took a couple steps forward. From his vantage point, the cave appeared to gradually narrow into a small tunnel, which eventually led upward to what he assumed was a rear exit behind the ridge. Although he and Brad hadn't specifically discussed it, he decided in that split second not to pursue the rebel.

As soon as Ostrigamo was out of sight, Brad rushed to Jessica's side. He helped her sit up and put her bound hands out in front of her. She looked beautiful and defiant despite her dirty face and the angry red slap mark on her cheek. Her long, blonde hair was matted and filthy. Her body shook as he untied her arms and ankles. As he did so, she rubbed her wrists, and he could see where the ropes had bitten into her skin leaving her raw and bloodied.

"Hi cousin," she said weakly, though with a big smile. "I thought you would never get here. I told that bastard you'd be coming for me, but he still wouldn't let me go." Her face clouded. "He's got something going on with my dad."

"I know," said Brad, "your dad is here."

"My dad is here? Where?"

"He was right outside with Jared. But they may already be on the move to the river. You can talk to him in a minute, when we're out of danger. But we gotta get moving."

"I'm not sure I ever want to talk to him again," Jessica said. "He's the whole reason we're in this mess. I've had several days to think. And I might be done with him."

Brad couldn't disagree, but he'd always been the peacekeeper, the diplomat. "Don't say that. You just need some time to cool off. He cared enough about getting you back to ask me to retrieve you."

"Retrieve me? Those were his exact words, weren't they? Everything is a transaction with him. A business deal. So cold and calculating. It'd be super great if just once he could say that he was worried about his daughter."

Brad knelt next to her and put his arm around her. "I hear you. But really. We've got to get out of here." He stood and extended his hand to her.

"I hate to break up this party," Ving said, standing over them and smiling. "But we need to run. The soldiers that are left are trying to regroup and it sounds like Ostrigamo's reinforcements are about to get here." While Ving was talking, Brad ducked behind Jessica and seemed to be searching the cave floor for something.

"I'm not leaving without some of these damned diamonds," Jessica protested. She started to scoop them up, but Brad grabbed her.

"There's no time!" he shouted. "We have to get out of here now!"

Before they could even take a step, Ostrigamo and four of his fresh troop reinforcements emerged from the tunnel at the back of the cave and opened fire.

"Let's go!" Brad yelled. He grabbed Jessica's hand and urged her to get up. She tried but stumbled and fell back on the cold floor of the cave. He scooped her up the best he could and helped her up. After a few steps, she got her footing back and seemed steadier on her feet.

The three of them raced out of the cave and into the chaos out front. Most of Ostrigamo's original force was down, and there were smashed and broken bodies scattered all over, but reinforcements were closing in from both sides. The sound of gunfire was deafening. Brad saw the Mbuti and their elephants fleeing into the jungle. He wanted to yell at them to stop, to come back and help. But it was no use. His voice wouldn't carry over the gunfire and both the animals and people looked terrified as they escaped.

Brad, Jessica and Ving ran for the river as fast as they could, but it was a losing effort. A hail of bullets rained all around them and Brad did his best to keep his body between Jessica and the gunmen, although he knew it wouldn't have mattered. If he got hit, even if he were shielding her, she'd go down too.

He imagined the feel of the bullets striking his back, preparing himself as best he could. He pictured himself as a sheet of steel that would protect his cousin from any harm. He kept running, zigzagging and supporting Jessica, urging her on. The sight of Jared, Pete and Jack popping out of the jungle at the trailhead in front of them to provide covering fire filled him with relief. It was just the break they needed. Brad thought he felt Jessica pick up speed when they saw her father, but it also felt like she was pulling Brad away from her dad.

All six of them hit the Bongou River trail at a dead run with the rebel reinforcements and Ostrigamo not far behind them. The incoming fire continued, but Pete managed to keep their pursuers from getting close enough to aim well enough to hurt them.

"The pirogues!" Brad yelled as they raced away. Pete waved a hand at him and slipped into the jungle beside the trail.

"I can't believe I'm leaving without my diamonds," Jessica gasped as she fled down the trail. "That is my diamond mine, I discovered it."

"Forget the diamonds. You're lucky to be alive. Just be glad you're getting out with your skin intact." Brad wasn't winded, but he wasn't about to argue with his stubborn cousin until they were safe. He could hear the gunfire getting more distant as Pete delayed the pursuing soldiers. Brad knew they only had minutes to get downriver to the boats and head to safety.

The five of them got to the water, and Jack stopped and bent over at the waist with his hands on his knees. "I just need a minute," he said, holding up his finger. "All this running." After a few seconds, he straightened. "Okay. I'm good now."

"So happy to hear that," Ving said. "Now can we get the hell out of here?"

"Wait," Jack said, approaching his daughter, as if he'd just realized his daughter was safe and standing in front of him. He strode up to her but didn't touch her. "Jessica." He held out his hands and Brad thought he was going to hug her. He'd never seen his Uncle Jack show any kind of affection before. But Jack grabbed Jessica by the shoulders and shook her. "What the hell were you thinking? You could have gotten yourself killed. You could have gotten us all killed."

Jessica pulled away from him and flicked his hands off her shoulders. "You're the last person who should be lecturing me or anyone. What the hell, Dad? Are you in bed with that monster who's been holding me like a stray dog all week?"

Jack's body stiffened. His daughter had never challenged him like this before. "We can talk about this later. All that matters right now is that you're safe." He forced her into a hug for several seconds and then let go. He took a step back. "You look like hell," he said, picking up her wrists and inspecting the abrasions.

"Gee thanks," she said, patting down her hair. "And here I thought I was going to win a beauty pageant."

"I hate to break up this touching moment," Brad said. "But we've got to get out of here. So everyone, please . . . listen up. We've got to get to the junction of the Bongou and Kotto Rivers."

"Isn't that where we saw those two pirogues pulled up on the beach?" Ving asked.

"Sure is," Brad said.

When Brad explained what he intended to do, Ving groaned "you mean I have to get back in one of those small boats on the river?" Jack and Jessica had stared at them in confusion until Jared explained about Ving's adventure with the hippo.

The two chuckled with delight at Jared's explanation, even though they were still in jeopardy. The anecdote lightened the mood and all of them felt a little better for the humor.

Brad only half listened as Jared talked. "We only have two small pirogues and I'm not sure the six of us will fit in them. At the very best, it will be a tight squeeze."

"Well, I guess we all better suck it in because these boats are our only hope," Ving said. "They're the only way to get to the Kotto then to the Ubangi and eventually down the Ubangi through the rapids to Mobaye. What other choice do we have?"

Brad looked entirely too calm as he spoke. "Just hear me out. You are right. I was trying to think of an alternative to the pirogues, but I think they're our best bet. Once we get to Mobaye, we will commandeer an aircraft that Pete can fly high enough and fast enough to avoid the SA-7 missiles the M23 had acquired from the Russians."

Jack interrupted. "Why not just paddle all the way to Bangui and take the truck. You know, the one that mysteriously disappeared from my salvage yard?" He caught the look on Brad's face and said to him, "Yeah, don't think I didn't know about that."

"There was a Huey parked in the smaller hangar at the airstrip in Mobaye," Jared added.

Brad held up his hand to silence Jack. "At normal cruising altitude the Huey would be a sitting duck for the small shoulder-fired surface-to-air missiles. But if Pete flies nap-of-the-earth, we have a chance. When a helicopter flies at treetop level, it's virtually impossible to tell which direction it's coming from or how fast it's flying. It reduces the likelihood of a missile hit to a very low percentage unless the pilot is foolish enough to hover or slow down to make an insertion. And I just don't see Pete doing any hovering." It wasn't the best of plans, but it was all he could come up with. The important thing was to keep their confidence level high so he could keep Jessica and Jack enthusiastic. He looked to Ving and Jared. The three shared a knowing glance. For all three of them knew what a small chance it was that this plan would be successful.

"Just one more question, how in the world are you going to *commandeer* this aircraft?" Jack asked.

Jared flashed Jack a cocky smile. "No need for you to worry about that. Just leave it to us."

*   *   *

 They reached the Bongou-Kotto River junction faster than any of them thought they would. "So far so good," Brad exclaimed as they came upon the two pirogues, still grounded on the beach. "Be careful getting in. With so many of us, it'll be way too easy for them to capsize. And believe me, none of us wants to go swimming with the hippos again." They piled in and waited anxiously for Pete to catch up. They heard him exchanging gunfire with their pursuers just up the trail.

Moments later, they watched as Pete approached them at a dead run, panting and red faced. Brad knew with Pete in sight that the rebels were moments behind. If they didn't get out of there in the next thirty seconds, they might all be dead. "Come on, Pete!" he yelled, urging him on. "We gotta go!"

Pete charged into the water. "Shove off!" he cried. He caught up to the second boat in waist-deep water just before it entered the swift current. Jack and Jared dragged him over the gunnel and he scrambled to sit upright. He took a deep breath, glanced over his shoulder at the shore and they were off. "Here they come! The rebels. They're right behind us." But the pirogues accelerated into the current and were out of range and around the bend before the angry and disappointed rebels reached the beach. In a fury, they began firing wildly, even though it was fruitless. The rounds splashed uselessly into the water behind the pirogues.

Brad, Jessica, and Ving led the way in the first boat. Still exhausted and slightly astounded that she'd actually been rescued, Jessica sat mutely on the floor between the benches while Brad and Ving navigated the waters. The Kotto River was smaller than the Ubangi but the current was faster. The rebels, racing down the river trail on foot, were never able to get within range. She turned to look at the angry men. "Where's Ostrigamo?" she asked Brad. "Shouldn't he be leading his men?"

"Cowards never do."

RUN FOR IT

Brad had no doubt that Ostrigamo had radioed ahead to his troops in Mobaye to be prepared for them, but he didn't mention it to Jack or Jessica. He knew Ving, Pete, and Jared would have thought of it too, though.

They reached the Ubangi River faster than they expected and headed downstream toward Mobaye. The rapids seemed rougher than Brad remembered, and the pirogues began to pitch about wildly. Jessica forced herself upright and held tight to the bench in front of her. She'd always had a solid stomach on the water, but now she was feeling sick. But, after all her cousin had gone through to rescue her, she wasn't about to complain. Unlike the boats they came upstream in, these were propelled by paddle power and the current. Brad had his hands full trying to guide the long, slender boat through the rapids.

"Not again!" Ving bellowed, gripping the gunnels tightly with his huge hands. "I am not getting pitched into the water with those people-eating dinosaurs again. Keep to the right, it's smoother there."

"I'm trying," Brad snapped. "These aren't exactly good conditions. Would you like to steer the boat?"

Ving, as massive of a man as he was, couldn't find his balance when he tried to stand up. "You're doing a great job," he said, trying not to smile. Just get us Mobaye in one piece.

"This is fun!" Jessica yelled over the roar of the rushing water, although she didn't think it was fun at all. She was trying to put up a good front for the men. Although her mood had lightened considerably since the men had liberated her from Ostrigamo. "What are you guys stressing about?"

"The hippos!" Brad and Ving said at the same time. Brad laughed in spite of himself. Even while occupied with keeping the pirogue centered in the deepest part of the rapids, the image of a spluttering and terrified Ving being chased by a pissed off hippo was funny . . . now.

Pete was having just as much trouble controlling the second pirogue, but he was keeping up with them. A few times he yelled out "Mayday" but then righted the boat and kept moving down river. Fifteen frantic minutes later, the two boats cleared the rapids and drifted smoothly into the swift, calm current. As the water leveled out, Jessica began to feel better.

They glided downriver, making good time. Their racing blood slowed and all of them felt the uneasy calm, certain it was temporary. "So what happens when we get to Mobaye?" Jessica asked. She'd been listening when Jared and Brad explained the plan, but she was too amped up and nervous to sit in silence now.

"Well, that depends on who or what is waiting for us," Brad told her. "Best case scenario is we find an aircraft and get the hell out of here."

"And worst case?" she asked.

"You don't want to know." Brad let his last comment sit in the air for a moment, then he said," Ving, check our position. I want to go ashore about a mile upstream of Mobaye."

"What and miss the rebel welcoming party?" he replied.

Brad chuckled at Ving's warped sense of humor. "Absolutely! We want to slip around the perimeter of the town and get to the airstrip, hopefully without having to engage any of Ostrigamo's buddies. Or you know, Ostrigamo himself. He's one slippery son of a bitch. There's no telling where he might be."

Ving checked the grid coordinates on the GPS and compared them to the acetate-covered map he had unfolded and laid across his lap. "Okay, we should be approaching a small slough about a mile from Mobaye just around that next bend up ahead. It'll be on the right in about," he checked his watch, trying to calculate how fast they were going, "seven minutes."

Jessica didn't know exactly what she was looking for, but that didn't stop her from surveying their surroundings. The jungle on the sides of the river was lush and green and so thick she was sure a few feet into it it'd be dark as night. Despite the circumstances of her being in the old, rickety boat on a hippo-infested river, she recognized the beauty of that part of the world. She closed her eyes so she'd always remember the moment. It was as exhilarating as it was terrifying.

"Good, keep your eyes peeled for a nice sandy beach where we won't have any trouble grounding the boats," said Brad.

Ving grunted and focused on the riverbank.

"Sandy beach?" Jessica asked. "The shore is either rock or jungle. Are you sure there is a sandy part?" Brad's request was much more difficult than it seemed; most of the time the jungle crowded up to the edge of the river and actually hung out over it. Bare spots were rare.

"Let's hope so," Brad muttered. "Otherwise getting out of here is going to be a trick."

About five minutes later, Ving spotted a short stretch of flat sandy beach at the same time Brad did, and he picked up a paddle from the floor of the boat to help him navigate out of the current. As soon as they were in shallow enough water, Jessica jumped out of the pirogue and guided its bow toward the beach. The water, although warm, stung her cuts and scrapes a bit. All of them were eager to get back on dry land, and they took no time at all to unass the pirogues and gather their gear. The vast majority of it had been left behind at the cave, so there wasn't much to carry.

Brad, Jessica and Ving stood on the beach waiting for the second pirogue to approach. As soon as it got close, the three of them rushed into the water and guided it to the beach. They held it steady while Jared, Jack and Pete got out. The six of them went back up the beach to catch their breath.

After a minute, Brad tried to rally his team. "I know we're all tired, but we can't stop now. All we need to do is make it to the outskirts of town and then to the airstrip. Everyone ready?"

"Brad," Jessica gasped, "I can't remember the last time I ate or drank anything. I'm starting to feel a little nauseous. Does anyone have any water?"

Ving pulled his pack off his shoulder. He opened it and retrieved two canteens. He handed one to Jessica and the other to Jack. "This is all we have until we get out of here. Let's make it last." They passed the canteens around until everyone had gotten some water.

"We good now?" Brad asked as he collected the containers and put them back in the canvas bag. "Let's head to town."

As they headed away from the water, they were traveling light and moving fast.

At first, they were extra cautious the closer they got to town. Being the middle of the day, all of them were certain they'd run into natives, and they had no way of knowing if they'd be as friendly as the pygmies or if they'd just as soon shoot them with poison darts. But the longer they went without encountering trouble, the braver and more confident they became. Once they came upon the small town, they could both see and hear townspeople speaking a foreign language. Brad and his team skirted the small village warily, and they approached the airstrip. The scorched wreckage of the Caribou had not been touched; the pieces scattered all over the ground in front of the damaged hangar. Brad was hoping against hope they'd find another transport, something better suited than the Huey. Maybe even another Caribou, but deep inside he believed that was a pipe dream. He was mentally preparing himself for a wild chopper ride through jungle country jammed full of missile-toting rebels.

The group walked purposefully through the wreckage and junk looking for something, anything that would be less risky than the helicopter. Ving kept picking up rusted parts—a rotor here and a piece of sheet metal there and laying them in a pile. Brad half thought his friend was going to build a flying machine as the rest of them looked on. He continued to watch Ving for a few more moments, thankful that he'd had the foresight to call his old buddy. Then he got back to searching the yard.

He rounded the corner, hoping to find something behind the building and was astounded when he spotted a gleaming new CASA C-212 Aviocar tied down beside the hangar. The odd looking, flat-bottomed, twin engine short takeoff and landing capable aircraft was ideal for remote jungle airstrips. Before he could even get excited about his seemingly miraculous find, he spotted three armed guards posted around the aircraft, and they seemed to be alert. Brad grunted. Word had gotten out and they were expected.

Ving came up beside Brad and said, "What are the chances? We're in desperate need of a way out of here and this thing appears like a phoenix rising from the ashes. Does it feel too perfect to you?"

"I wouldn't call three armed guards perfect. But it does seem suspect."

Pete joined them. "Do you think Ostrigamo set this up?"

Brad eyed him. "Like had this plane delivered so we would find it and get ambushed while we try to lift it?"

"Something like that."

Brad was starting to get a sense of Ostrigamo and how he worked. "I do think he planted the plane.

No one is this lucky. But I can't figure out why the guards aren't hiding. Wouldn't it make more sense for them to hide inside the aircraft and shoot us when we tried to board?"

"Who cares," Ving said. "It's here. We're here. We're armed. Three stupid soldiers are the only things standing between us and being on our way home to sunny and not so hot Texas. Let's do this."

They started to walk away but Brad stopped and turned to Pete. "Can you fly that?" he asked.

"It's got wings, don't it?" Pete said wryly. "If it's got wings, brother, I can fly it." He grinned. "Of course, it might be a little scary at first; I'll have to get familiar with the controls while we're flying. I've never even been inside one of those."

"Shit, maybe we'll get lucky and they'll have left the keys and the flight manual on the driver's seat," Brad said. They shared a grin only men who had survived the totally unpredictable vagaries and dangers of war would understand. The bond and the sick humor were entirely incomprehensible to those who had never been there.

"Semper Fi!" Brad said quietly.

"Oorah!" Pete replied, with a look of respect.

Brad motioned for the others to circle around him. "Okay guys, let's keep this clean and simple," he said to them as they gathered in a huddle in the shade of the building. "We need to take this aircraft quick and take off before all Ostrigamo's people decide to show up. I don't want any stray bullets hitting our plane. Jack, you and Jared hang back here with Jessica. Just wait for my signal." He took a deep breath. "When we get into position, Ving, you take the man on the far left. Pete, you take the guy on the far right, I'll take the one in the middle." He glanced at the three unsuspecting, but prepared guards. They were all armed with weapons he knew could take down the plane. Then he turned his attention back to the huddle.

"Everybody got it?" They all nodded, serious now. "Let's do this." They split up and Brad and his back up headed toward the hangar.

"Wait," Jessica said, her voice too loud and a bit desperate. Brad stopped and let out an impatient breath. "Thank you." She threw her arms around his neck. "For everything. Be careful." And then she let go and turned away with Jack and Jared.

Brad, Ving and Pete advanced silently, using the hangar for cover. They tried to enter the hangar through the same rear entrance they had used before, but it was secured, a reinforced door and a heavy chain keeping them out. Undaunted, Brad gave hand signal instructions and Pete began to slowly circle around the right side of the hangar while Ving and Brad crept around the left side.

As soon as they were in position, Brad counted down from three to one using his fingers. When he dropped his hand, he took aim and initiated the assault by taking the first shot. Pete and Ving responded to the signal when they heard Brad's shot ring out. The three guards were on the ground in a matter of seconds and Pete took off toward the aircraft. He weaved his way around the bodies and was inside the aircraft while they were still bleeding. He sat in the cockpit and took a moment to take in the controls. *It's an aircraft,* he told himself. *You can fly anything.* Then he performed a hasty preflight check and located the controls. He was right. It was just a plane. Different from anything he'd ever flown before, but he knew he could do this.

Brad, in the meantime, was waving frantically toward Jessica, Jack and Jared, urging them to run to the plane while Ving kept an eye on the road from Mobaye. None of them harbored any doubt that the gunfire had been heard by the rebel forces, and it was only a matter of minutes before they'd have unwelcomed company. Brad helped his cousin, uncle and friend board the aircraft, then he got in.

"We've got less than half a tank of fuel," Pete reported when Brad boarded.

"Is that enough to get us to Gemena?"

"Multiple vehicles approaching from town," Ving shouted through the entry door. He'd be the last to board after he made sure the aircraft was ready for flight.

"It's gonna have to be," Pete yelled, flipping the switch for the port engine. He pushed a button and the engine sputtered to life, running roughly. He needed to wait for it to smooth out, but there was no time. Flipping the switch for the starboard engine, he pressed the starter button. "Load 'em up!" he screamed to Brad over the roar of the engines as he moved the throttles toward the emergency power quadrant. The engines did their own screaming as they smoothed out and began to roar.

Jack and Jessica scrambled into their seats as Ving chopped the tie downs with his fighting knife. He dove through the door and Jared, who'd been waiting for him, pulled the entry door closed behind him with his left hand. He was still favoring his right arm. Before the door was even locked, Pete began to taxi toward the grassy runway. Rebel vehicles filled with troops drove off the road from town and onto the grass strip, the soldiers standing in the backs of the trucks firing wildly at the plane as it bounced down the airstrip.

Pete slammed the throttles all the way to the stops and began to pray as the craft gathered speed. Three rebel trucks were drawing closer and Brad felt more than heard the bullets piercing the fuselage.

"Get us the hell out of here, Pete!" Brad yelled. He looked down and saw Ostrigamo standing up in the back of a Jeep aiming a high-powered rifle at the plane. As the aircraft gained altitude and was safely out of reach of the rebel and his thugs, Brad smiled and waved.

There wasn't much life in the controls yet, but Pete yanked back on the yoke and the C-212 bounced twice and lifted off the ground.

"We're lucky this is a short takeoff and landing aircraft," Pete snapped. "A few more seconds on the ground and we would have been Swiss cheese."

Their relief was short-lived. Pete caught sight of a trail of smoke out of the corner of his eye and jerked the yoke, sending the plane into a steep bank to the right to avoid the SA-7 missile. Jack let out an involuntary yelp as the missile whizzed by the plane. It exploded in the air several meters away from the aircraft. The burst almost sent the plane hurtling out of control to the ground, but Pete's quick response righted them again.

Several warhead fragments had hit the right engine and it started to smoke and sputter. Pete feathered the prop and then shut down the engine. He had to make a correction to maintain a level flight path, but he managed it after a fashion. He banked the craft gently and guided them slowly toward the DRC. There were no more missiles. They crossed the Ubangi and entered DRC airspace.

"Good news, folks," he yelled above the roar of the engines. "I'm sure the smoke was a dead giveaway that we lost an engine. But the remaining one is running strong. I believe we will reach Gemena safe and sound." *That is,* he thought, *if we don't run out of fuel.* He began to pray.

"What happens when we get this bird on the ground?" Jack asked.

"We?" Pete asked, then winked.

"Well, *we* need to get out of this country as soon as possible," Ving said, explaining the obvious. He held up a battered satellite phone. "I will contact my old military buddy, Hank Guzman, and with any luck, he'll arrange for an emergency military transport out of Gemena and back to the U.S."

"You make it sound so easy," Jack said.

"It's the expensive way to travel, but we don't have any other choice than to get the hell out of here. So we'd better make it as easy as possible. Now if you'll excuse me, I need to make a phone call and get us an escort out of this godforsaken place." He started punching numbers on the brick of a phone, effectively dismissing Jack.

"How long is the flight?" Jessica asked Brad.

"I don't know," he responded. "Let me ask Pete." Brad unbuckled his seatbelt and gently put his hand on Pete's shoulder, as to not startle him. "Jess wants to know how long we'll be in the air. She looks exhausted. I think she wants to know if she has time to nap."

"About two hours," Pete said. "But good luck sleeping."

"What do you—" The plane hit a pocket of turbulence that made Brad feel like his stomach was shooting up through his throat. It was the same feeling he'd gotten the first time he went on a six-loop rollercoaster called Phobia. "Oh that," he said, swallowing hard. "How long do you expect this rough air to last?"

"Just the two hours." Pete grinned.

Brad made his way back to Jessica, but she was already sleeping. *God bless her.* She looked exhausted. He could only imagine what she'd been through since Ostrigamo had captured her. Suddenly he had a sickening thought. What *had* she been through? And where were the two people she'd gone into the jungle with? Had that monster of a man touched his cousin? He felt sweat gathering at his temples just thinking about all the horrible things that could have happened to

Jessica in the last weeks. He'd been so focused on finding and rescuing her—that he hadn't allowed himself to think what she'd lived *through*.

He tried to close his eyes and block the thoughts that were now plaguing him from his mind. But it seemed as though every time he did, the little plane hit turbulence and he was jolted awake.

"Sorry to bother you folks, but if you look out the port side of the cabin, you'll see we're on our initial approach," Pete said, laughing at his attempt to sound like a commercial airline pilot. Jessica opened her eyes and stretched, and for a moment Brad thought she looked as if she'd forgotten where they were.

"Did Pete say we're almost there?" Jessica asked Brad.

"Sure did," he replied. 'Hey, I've got a question for you. What happened to the people you were with?

Surely you didn't go into the jungles of Africa alone."

"When Ostrigamo found us, he said he only wanted me because of my father. I guess he thought I was worth more to him than two research assistants. Kerry and James were released with our guides and told to get out of the CAR or face the consequences. I'll call them when we land, but I'm sure they're okay."

"Give me their last names and I'll call in a few favors to check on them. But . . . " He pretended to drop something and bent over, feeling around the floor under his seat. "What could this be?" He held up a package about the size of a baseball. He shook it and brought it to his ear. "Any guesses?"

"I don't know," Jessica said. "Can I hold it?"

He handed it across the aisle to her. "Why don't you just open it?"

She tore open the package. "Diamonds!" she shrieked as the rough stones spilled out into her hand. "How? Where? When did you get these?"

"Well, would you look at that? And you thought there was no time to collect them back in the cave." He reached across the space between them and plucked one from the pouch. He held it between his index finger and thumb. "I guess it's a good thing I scooped up a few while you and Ving were busy talking. I believe these are yours."

Jessica jumped out of her seat and lunged for him. She wrapped her arms around his neck. She squeezed him tightly, laughing ecstatically. "Thank you. Thank you. Thank you. I can't believe you did this for me. I can't believe you did all of this for me. Don't worry," she whispered. "I'm going to share them with you guys!"

"I don't give a damn about your diamonds, Jess," Brad whispered softly. "I'm just happy to have you back in one piece."

"Me too," she said. "Truth be told, I didn't think I was making it out alive. How can I ever thank you?"

"Just keep on being you, darlin'. Just keep on being you."

EPILOGUE – Day 7

Brad let out a huge sigh as the commercial jetliner landed smoothly at Dallas/Fort Worth International Airport. The mission had gone relatively well. They'd accomplished their objective and made it back with only one minor injury and zero fatalities. For a half-assed, hurry-up plan, it had been a remarkable success.

He always enjoyed the feeling of satisfaction he got at the completion of a successful mission, but this one had been special. This one had been personal, it had been for family. His cousin Jessica was the most important person in the world to him and it felt great to finally have her home safe. And his uncle owed him one. It was always a good day when Uncle Jack wasn't the one in control. His world was right again . . . and a share of Ostrigamo's diamonds was just icing on the cake.

THE END

Thank you for taking the time to read TRACK DOWN AFRICA. If you enjoyed it, please consider telling your friends or posting a short review. Word of mouth is an author's best friend and much appreciated. Thank you, Scott Conrad.

EXCLUSIVE SNEAK PEEK: TRACK DOWN ALASKA – BOOK 2

THE CRASH

18 April 1600 hours AKDT

The Piper PA-18-180 Super Cub banked hard to the right as the engine sputtered and quit. The altimeter indicator needle was spinning wildly with no place in sight to set the plane down.

Pete Sabrowski, a former Naval Aviator in the Marine Corps, glanced nervously at the Alaskan forest below. It was going to be a tree landing, and that didn't bode well for the passengers or the lightweight fabric and aluminum tube aircraft fuselage. The Piper is the perfect choice for flying

209

in the Alaskan bush. The Super Cub is well known for its ability to take off and land in incredibly short distances.

First generation Cubs were remarkable enough, but the modification that made it the current airplane of choice in the bush was the use of the Lycoming O-360 power plant. A high-lift wing placement design and the powerful one hundred and eighty horsepower engine made the Super Cub especially adaptable to either a floatplane or a ski plane. This aircraft could take off in as little as two hundred feet.

"Mayday, Mayday!" Sam Henderson, the charter pilot, spoke calmly into the microphone. "I say again, Mayday! This is *Snow Gopher*. Red Piper Super Cub. Engine failure, we're going down. Visibility poor, overshot destination. Best guess is we're just east of Mount Watana. Mayday, Mayday!"

There was no response.

In this part of Alaska, there were no air traffic controllers. He checked to see if the emergency location transmitter light was blinking. He thumped the switch once hard and the red light started flashing. There was an FAA monitoring station in Talkeetna, but if they were responding Henderson couldn't hear them. There was no other response.

Normally bush pilots listen for distress calls and respond or retransmit if they're near enough to pick up the SOS. Sam Henderson mentally berated himself for his poor choice in not turning back to Talkeetna when the weather went bad so quickly. He knew better than to chance it, but the Stephan Lake Lodge flight was a short one and he had flown it a thousand times.

It had seemed to him at the time no riskier to continue on to the lodge than to try to return to Talkeetna. Besides, there was a sweet little redhead at the lodge who usually made room in her bed for him when he landed there.

Visibility had gotten progressively worse and his chronometer told him he had missed Stephan Lake. They had been flying too long. He explained to Pete Sabrowski that he had overshot their destination and began a slow turn back to the southeast, dropping to the lowest level he dared, looking for a familiar landmark. That's when the carburetor iced over, and the engine sputtered to a stop.

"Shit, we're going in!" he barked ...

Visit the author at: ScottConradBooks.com

A Brad Jacobs Thriller Series by Scott Conrad:

TRACK DOWN AFRICA – BOOK 1

TRACK DOWN ALASKA – BOOK 2

TRACK DOWN AMAZON – BOOK 3

TRACK DOWN IRAQ – BOOK 4

TRACK DOWN BORNEO – BOOK 5

TRACK DOWN EL SALVADOR – BOOK 6

TRACK DOWN WYOMING – BOOK 7

TRACK DOWN THAILAND – BOOK 8